Whitebridge Nurse

ROSE DANA

THORNDIKE
CHIVERS

This Large Print edition is published by Thorndike Press®, Waterville, Maine USA and by BBC Audiobooks, Ltd, Bath, England.

Published in 2004 in the U.S. by arrangement with Maureen Moran Agency.

Published in 2004 in the U.K. by arrangement with the author.

U.S. Hardcover 0-7862-6530-2 (Candlelight)
U.K. Hardcover 0-7540-9657-2 (Chivers Large Print)
U.K. Softcover 0-7540-9658-0 (Camden Large Print)

The text of this Large Print edition is unabridged.
Other aspects of the book may vary from the original edition.

Set in 16 pt. Plantin by Ramona Watson.

Printed in the United States on permanent paper.

British Library Cataloguing-in-Publication Data available

Library of Congress Cataloging-in-Publication Data

Dana, Rose, 1912–
    Whitebridge nurse / by Rose Dana.
        p. cm.
    ISBN 0-7862-6530-2 (lg. print : hc : alk. paper)
    1. Parent and adult child — Fiction.   2. Children of physicians — Fiction.   3. Fathers and daughters — Fiction.
4. Divorced women — Fiction.   5. Hospitals — Fiction.
6. Nurses — Fiction.   7. Large type books.   I. Title.
PR9199.3.R5996W475 2004
    813′.54—dc22   2004045954

Whitebridge Nurse

To Irene Murray, friend and editor

CHAPTER ONE

The road sign said: "Whitebridge, five miles." Jane Weaver was familiar with the road and knew she would reach her father's house in less than ten minutes. It had been two years since she'd been home, and now that the moment of reunion with her father was near she began to feel uneasy. So much had happened since she'd last seen Whitebridge that she felt almost as if she were a different person returning.

It was an ideal time of year to come home. Early July was generally pleasant and warm in the White Mountain area of New Hampshire. And the annual invasion of summer residents and tourists created a lot of extra activity and social life. Whitebridge had no adjacent ski area, and so nearby communities gained most of the winter resort business. But summer was a busy time in the town, and as a result her father's medical practice usually tripled.

Jane was a doctor's daughter and a full-fledged nurse herself. Her mother had died in infancy, and she'd been brought up by her father's spinster sister, Emily, who still kept house for Jane's father. Indeed, it had been an urgent phone call from her Aunt Emily that had made Jane reluctantly decide to return to her home town.

Jane, who had been living in Boston and working at the Peter Bent Brigham, shared an apartment on Beacon Street with another nurse. The phone call from her aunt had come shortly after she'd returned to the apartment from the day shift at the hospital.

Aunt Emily had sounded as precise and anxious as usual. "Jane, I felt I simply must call you," the older woman told her over the line.

Jane recognized her aunt's tone as the one she always adopted when a crisis arose. Resignedly she asked, "What is it now, Aunt Emily?"

"I think you should come home. Your father is badly upset, and he needs you."

She at once began a retreat. "I'm sure that isn't so," she told her aunt.

"Yes, it is," her aunt insisted. "He isn't as young as he used to be, and things worry him more these days, especially since the trouble he's had with you. There is a major problem concerning the hospital."

"Oh!" Jane was interested. She knew her aunt was not a person to exaggerate, and if she implied there was a crisis it was all too likely to be a real one.

"The town council had another special session last night," Aunt Emily had continued in a worried tone. "And they've just about decided not to continue supporting the hospital. That would mean its closing."

Jane gasped. "Not after all these years!" She knew that her father had given his entire professional life to the people of Whitebridge and the surrounding rural area. He had helped design the Benson Memorial Hospital and been its head doctor in the nearly thirty years since it had first opened.

"I'm afraid they mean it this time," her aunt worried. "And you can imagine how badly your father feels about it. I hear him pacing in his room at nights."

"But surely with the shortage of doctors and hospitals these days, the town needs Benson Memorial," Jane protested.

"It isn't as simple as that," Aunt Emily said. "I think you should come back here and work with your father at the hospital for a while; let him know you care about him and his problems."

"I don't think I matter that much to him

any more." Jane was thinking of the one brief meeting they'd had since she had left Whitebridge. It had been in Boston after she'd gone back there to work. Her father had been in town for the day and had arranged to meet her for lunch. He had been friendly but reserved, and she'd gotten the impression there was still a great barrier between them. He had not forgiven her.

"Of course you matter to him," her aunt argued. "He needs you now. Don't let your pride keep you from helping him."

Jane sat down on the arm of the sofa and frowned into the receiver before replying. Then she asked, "How do I know he'd welcome me? Aren't you taking all this on yourself?"

"I am," her Aunt Emily admitted frankly. "But I know he misses you and would be glad to have you here. And the hospital is short a nurse. When can you come?"

"Not for a week," she said, "if I do decide to."

"That will have to do," the old woman said in her matter-of-fact way. "I had hoped you could make it sooner. But just as long as you do get here —"

Jane had put down the phone with a feeling of dismay and defeat. She'd not intended to return to Whitebridge under any conditions. Now her aunt had cleverly blackmailed her into it by stressing her father's need of her. And when it came to a showdown she couldn't really turn away from him. The bond between them was strong — so strong that only her marriage to Dick Grayson had caused the rift between them. It was almost three years since Dick had first come to Whitebridge as golf pro for the Whitebridge Country Club. Jane had been one of the first people to meet him, and she'd at once fallen for his good looks and easy charm of manner.

Dick was a six-foot, broad-shouldered outdoor man with bronzed good looks and curly blond hair. He courted her the entire summer, and when he left Whitebridge for his winter job in Florida he'd begged her to marry him and go with him. She'd refused then, but they'd corresponded and talked on the phone in the months that followed. And when he returned to Whitebridge their romance became more intense than ever.

It was that autumn she had agreed to marry him. She told her father and explained she'd be leaving Whitebridge and the hospital. While she'd felt he would be disappointed, she hadn't dreamed he would offer any active resistance to the match.

But he had! Raising his shaggy white eyebrows, he said, "But I took it for granted you'd be marrying Stephen Benson."

"Steve and I have been close friends," Jane had admitted. "But we don't really love each other." Steve had been her chief male companion since she'd come back to Whitebridge from nursing school. He was the manager of the Benson Shoe Factory, the town's only industrial plant, and his family had played a prominent part in Whitebridge through the years.

Benson money had done a great deal for the town. They were its wealthiest family, and an uncle of Steve Benson had left the trust fund for the hospital which bore the Benson name. Now there were only Steve, his younger sister, Sally, and their aging mother left of the clan. Jane liked Steve well enough for an odd evening out or a game of golf, but she'd never considered marrying him. The truth was that Steve had always seemed more like a thoughtful older brother to her. And she hadn't given any thought to marriage until Dick came along.

Her father's opinion of Dick had been completely unexpected. "He'll be no good for you," David Weaver predicted gloomily. "He's a potential alcoholic and will probably be unfaithful as well. The marriage won't last six months!"

As a matter of fact, her father was proven wrong. Somehow, in spite of almost constant wrangling, abuse and threats, she'd hung onto her marriage for eight months. At that time she realized it was no use. Dick didn't protest her suit for divorce, and within a short time she'd regained her freedom and legally taken her maiden name.

It had been an unhappy, degrading experience, but she determined it wouldn't ruin her life. So she'd gone to work in Boston. So far she'd been doing very well and had not had any desire to return to her home town.

Now Aunt Emily had talked her into coming home. Would it work out? She hoped so, since she did miss her father's company, but it worried her that the easy father and daughter relationship she'd known with him might never be the same again.

She was nearing the town itself now, with its thousand or so inhabitants. With the summer people, there would be at least three thousand in the immediate area, and the other small towns in the district would be equally swollen with summer traffic.

She slowed her small foreign sports car and took note of familiar landmarks.

She'd written only one of her friends of her exact time of arrival. And she hadn't had any letter in reply from Maggie Grant.

Maggie was certainly her best friend in Whitebridge. She taught in the local high school, and her father owned the only drugstore in the town. She and Jane had often gone to the Whitebridge Country Club together with their dates. At last word Maggie had still been going with a pleasant young man who was the principal of the school where she taught.

The traffic moved on, and she turned into the pleasant side street where her father's house was located. It was a big rambling building with verandahs front and side, large bay windows and elaborate shingled turrets gracing its upper story. It was in no particular style but had a comfortable appearance. Her father's office was located in what had once been the front parlor, and a sizable room across the hall from it served as a waiting room. The balance of the house was their private domain.

The slate-colored house sat on a small hill, and the driveway had quite a grade. As Jane drove up to it, she saw her father's car was not there, so she knew he must be out on calls. It was a little after four in the afternoon, and if he'd been having afternoon office hours his own car would have been there, along with the cars of patients parked in front of the house. All seemed quiet at the moment.

She drove up and parked by the side verandah. Then she got out and went to the side door without bothering to take her luggage from the car. By the time she reached the door Emily had opened it and was holding out her arms to embrace her.

"I've been worried sick for fear you'd changed your mind," Aunt Emily said, holding Jane tightly against her and kissing her on the cheek. She was a big, bony woman with a pleasant if somewhat plain face.

Jane laughed ruefully. "Maybe I should have. I've been getting terribly nervous, worrying about how Father would receive me."

"You needn't worry," Aunt Emily said with a twinkle in her eyes. "I mentioned at noon you were coming, and I could tell he was pleased."

"I hope so." Jane sighed and glanced around the living room to see if it had changed any. It hadn't. The old but good

15

pieces of furniture were all in their familiar places, and it even had the same spicy, pungent smell that somehow seeped in from the office and which she would always associate with it. She smiled at her aunt. "It looks just the same."

"I keep it clean even if it's not stylish," Aunt Emily said.

"It seems so long ago since I left!"

"Let's not talk about that," Aunt Emily said, "and especially not in front of your father. Lord knows, he has plenty of other things to bother him these days without bringing that up."

"I'll be careful," Jane promised.

"We'll get your things and put them in your room," Aunt Emily said. "Then we can sit down to talk over a cup of tea."

They went out to the car and between them carried in the bags. Then Aunt Emily led her upstairs to her old room. Jane let out a pleased cry when she saw that it was freshly painted.

"I like this ivory shade," she said, standing in the middle of her beloved room and staring around. The big bed had its same pink cover with ruffles, and even her own doll sat proudly resting against a fancy pillow. She went over and cuddled the long-gowned doll in her arms. Her eyes shining, she told her aunt, "It is good to be back! I'm glad you made me come."

Her aunt's plain face showed a smile. "I hope you'll go on thinking that." And then, as if suddenly remembering, she added, "Maggie Grant phoned and said she'd drop by as soon as she finished at school."

"Good! I wrote her, but she didn't answer."

"She mentioned that and apologized," Aunt Emily said. "She sounded happy you were coming home."

Jane carefully returned the doll to the pillow. "We were very close friends. I hope we can continue to be."

"It's your father I'm worried about," her aunt said with a sigh. "Let's go on down to our tea, and I'll tell you."

When they were seated in the living room over afternoon tea, Aunt Emily began to pour out her tale of woe. "If the hospital is closed, I think your father will feel he has failed in his life's work," she said.

Cup in hand, Jane frowned. "But why should the town want to close the Benson Memorial? Didn't old Mr. Benson leave a trust fund to operate it?"

"It pays only a portion of the upkeep today. The town has to pay the balance.

Both Winchester and Dunstan have local hospitals, and neither of these towns is twenty miles away. People in both those places are faced with the same problem we have here. They try to support their own hospitals as well as they can, so we don't get any of them." She paused. "The truth is that the big new hospital and clinic at Bladeworth is taking the majority of the patients from this entire district. Bladeworth is only an hour's drive by car, and they have the latest facilities."

"They were just finishing the building when I left," Jane recalled.

"When it opened the trouble began," Aunt Emily said. "Not that your father doesn't treat a good many patients. He does. But there are too many beds empty for the cost of operation. Or at least that's what the town council thinks."

"So what do they propose to do?"

"They have been in touch with the trust company that looks after the estate and have asked them to investigate the possibility of the money being paid annually to the new hospital at Bladeworth for the benefit of Whitebridge people."

Jane sat back in her chair. "I can't see them allowing that."

"So far they haven't given a reply."

18

"And what would they do about the hospital itself?"

Aunt Emily shrugged. "Sell it for some other purpose and add the money to the trust fund, though I can't see them getting rid of a building that size here. It isn't suitable for a factory and we don't need another hotel, certainly not in that location."

"Then it looks as if they will have to continue with the hospital," Jane suggested.

"I wouldn't count on that," the older woman said, filling her teacup a second time. "Steve Benson is our new mayor, and he's dead set on saving the town money. If there's a way to shut the hospital, he'll find it."

Jane speculated, "But what about emergency cases?"

"Your father has pointed that out. Only a local hospital can really take care of a true emergency. Their answer to that is that we don't have that many emergencies."

Putting down her cup, Jane sighed. "In other words, they've made up their minds they want a change."

"That's the size of it."

"Whom does Father have with him on the hospital staff now?" Jane asked.

"Just two other doctors. Your father does most of the surgery himself. Then there is

Dr. Wallace Milton, who took over old Dr. Silverwood's practice in Northville. He uses the hospital and sometimes serves as anesthetist in serious operations. Otherwise your father has Miss McCumber on the anesthesia machine."

"She's still head nurse?"

Her aunt nodded. "Yes. And at the moment she hasn't much help. That's why you'll come in so handy."

"If I decide to stay," Jane said with a knowing look.

"But you must!" Aunt Emily insisted. "There's a new doctor in Rangely since you've left. He bought the old Logie place and set up an office in it. His name is Boyd Davis. He's a bachelor, and his mother is keeping house for him. Your father likes him and is glad to have him bring his patients to the hospital."

"It sounds as if he has two good men to help him then," Jane said. "And they should be enough for the number of patients Benson Memorial is handling."

"Your father would like to see a doctor on duty at the hospital around the clock," her aunt said. "But a forty-bed hospital hardly qualifies as a training institution, so there are not likely to be any interns or residents."

"Dad has given an awful lot of himself to the hospital."

"More than even you can guess," Aunt Emily said decidedly. "He'll be heartbroken if it closes. And that is why I thought you should be here to give him what comfort and support you can."

Jane smiled wryly. "I'm afraid I haven't given him much comfort so far."

"Anyone can make an unfortunate marriage," her aunt said with a serious expression on her plain face. "You shouldn't dwell on it so. That part of your life is behind you. You made a mistake, and luckily you were able to correct it. You must try to do better in the future."

Jane listened humbly to the modest sermon. While she might have resented such plain speech from a stranger, it was all right coming from Aunt Emily. She had been foolish, and she'd paid a price in unhappiness for it. Now she must try to forget it.

"If Dad wants me to stay, I will," she said quietly.

"I'm sure he'll be delighted," Aunt Emily said. "And so will a lot of other people, including young Mayor Steve Benson. He always asks about you."

Mention of Steve's name brought a

blush to Jane's cheeks. She said, "I thought he'd have married by now."

Her aunt smiled. "I don't think he ever got over you jilting him."

"But I didn't jilt him," Jane protested. "We were just friends."

"I wonder if that's what Steve thought? I'm sure his feelings for you went much deeper than yours did for him."

Jane was anxious to change the subject. So she quickly asked, "What about his sister, Sally?"

"She's living back here again," Aunt Emily said with a look of disapproval. "She spent a while in New York, but I guess it didn't suit her. Since she's been back, she's set her cap for Dr. Wallace Milton."

Jane arched an eyebrow. "That's the bachelor? The one whose mother keeps house for him in Rangely?"

Her aunt shook her head. "No, that's Dr. Boyd Davis. You're getting the two confused. The one Sally is interested in is Dr. Wallace Milton in Northville. And the awful part about it is he already has a wife."

Jane opened her eyes wide. "I didn't think Sally would try anything like that here."

"Well, she is the town's richest girl, and

pretty in her way. I suppose she thinks she can have who she likes. And Dr. Milton's wife is not well. She's a neurotic who rarely leaves their house. The one or two times she's attended a social function in town she's behaved rather badly."

"Badly?"

"She has an acid tongue and she's terribly jealous of her husband," Aunt Emily explained. "She seems on the defensive all the time, and there's no need for it. As a result, the local people have nothing to do with her."

"Sounds like an unhappy situation."

Aunt Emily nodded. "Believe me, it is. So maybe that's why Sally thought she could capture the doctor. To give him credit, he has paid her hardly any attention."

"But Sally is keeping after him?"

"Yes," Aunt Emily said. "So maybe she'll cause another scandal in this poor old town yet."

Jane smiled thinly. "I have an idea this poor old town thrives on scandal."

Her aunt got up to take the teapot out to the kitchen. "It's such a small place, everyone is looking over his neighbor's fence."

"Peeking over would be a better description," Jane suggested as she also rose to take the rest of the things on the tray. As she followed her aunt out, she asked, "What time do you think Dad will get back?"

"Around about six, I expect," Aunt Emily said. "That's about his usual time."

Jane helped her aunt wash the few dishes and then went back to the living room. While she was standing there, a car drove up into the driveway next to her car.

Her aunt beamed. "That will be Maggie Grant on her way from school."

A moment later there was a light knock on the door, and when Jane opened it Maggie came in with a laughing greeting and hugged her. Maggie was Jane's own age, a striking blonde with her hair in bangs at the front and shoulder length.

"Jane! It's so good to have you back," Maggie said happily.

"You're the person I was most eager to see."

"And I felt the same about you," the other girl said. "There's no one I've ever missed as I did you when you left White-bridge."

Jane grimaced. "Well, I have to come back."

"Our good luck," Maggie said. "I'm on

my way over to Rangely to a school district meeting."

"Are you and your principal still dating?" Jane asked.

It was Maggie's turn to crimson. "No," she said. "He left a year ago. I've been playing the field since."

Jane raised her eyebrows. "No one special?"

"Not really," Maggie said with a resigned smile on her lovely face. "I suppose my best friend these days is Dr. Boyd Davis. He's taking me over to Rangely now."

"The new doctor," Jane said. "And a bachelor! Is he nice?"

Maggie nodded. "He's one of the finest young men I've ever known. But I repeat, we're just good friends."

Jane smiled. "It sounds like a wonderful beginning."

"I wouldn't count on it," Maggie said with a hint of bitterness. "Would you like to meet him before we leave?"

"I would."

"Come on out then," Maggie said, glancing at her wristwatch and starting for the door. "I daren't keep him waiting any longer."

"When will you have time for a talk?" Jane asked, following her out.

"Maybe later tonight or tomorrow

night," Maggie said. "I'll phone you."

The blonde girl crossed the verandah and went to a gray sedan parked almost abreast of Jane's car. Jane followed her and came to a halt by the driver's window.

As the driver put the window down, Maggie said, "Jane, I'd like you to meet Dr. Boyd Davis, a colleague of your father's."

It took all the poise at Jane's command to cover her surprise. For the handsome man smiling politely at her from behind the wheel was a Negro.

CHAPTER TWO

"I've looked forward to meeting you, Jane," Boyd Davis said. He was wearing a conservative sports coat and a white shirt with a brown tie. He looked neat and professional as he got out of the car and shook hands with her.

"I just heard about you opening a practice in Rangely," Jane finally managed with some grace. "They needed a g.p. badly. How do you feel about the hospital?"

The young man spoke earnestly. "I have found it a great help. Your father has been wonderful to my patients. But as you probably know, the town is divided about the hospital."

"I've only learned that in the last hour," she said. "I guess it will take me some time to catch up on everything."

Maggie gave her a knowing smile. "I'll help as much as I can."

"I'm sure you will," Jane agreed, returning her smile. Maggie went around to take her place in the front seat, and the young Negro doctor closed the door after her. As he came to get behind the wheel again, Jane added, "I'm glad we've met. I hope I see you again soon."

"I look forward to that." He smiled as he started the car. "Miss McCumber will be happy to have another nurse on the staff."

Jane stood in the driveway as they backed into the street. Maggie waved as they drove away, and Jane waved back. Then she went on into the house. Aunt Emily was standing in the living room waiting for her.

"Well, you met him," she said.

Jane gave her a reproachful look. "You didn't tell me!"

"That he was a Negro? I didn't think it was important, I guess. I'd just started to fill you in."

"Maggie didn't say anything either." Jane gave her aunt a worried look. "Just how serious is this thing between them?"

Aunt Emily seemed placid. "They go out together occasionally. A few loose tongues have wagged, but that's about par for Whitebridge. He's a very nice young man, and Maggie is a sensible girl. I'm sure they both realize the problems they face."

"If Dr. Davis is good enough to doctor the people in town, he should be good enough to take Maggie out," Jane suggested.

"That's exactly how I feel," Aunt Emily said. "And I'm certain Maggie thinks the same way."

"Still, I wouldn't want to see either of them hurt," Jane worried. "And that could happen if they should fall in love."

The older woman raised her eyebrows. "I've privately asked myself if that mightn't have happened already. But as I said before, they're both smart young people. I don't think they'll allow it to go that far."

Jane offered her a forlorn look. "I thought I was intelligent, and consider the trap I fell into."

"I wouldn't worry about Maggie," her aunt said. "Or Dr. Davis either. Your father will tell you he's a fine young man."

Jane went upstairs to unpack and change for the evening meal. She had barely finished and gotten into a dark jersey dress when she heard the door open downstairs and her father's booming voice as he talked with Aunt Emily. She quickly put on the finishing touches of her make-up and went down to greet him.

He was standing with the folded evening newspaper in one hand when she entered the living room. She thought he looked

29

worn and thinner than he had been when she had had lunch with him in Boston. He was a tall, aristocratic-looking man with a mane of snow white hair and heavy matching eyebrows. His face brightened when he saw her, and he went to meet her and took her in his arms with deep affection.

After he'd touched his lips to her forehead, he gave her a fond glance. "So you finally decided to come back?"

"Aunt Emily sort of twisted my arm," she told him.

Her father continued smiling. "Well, I'm glad she did. We've missed you more than you know."

They walked over to the divan by the window and sat down together. She gave her father another appraising glance. "You don't look well," she told him.

He showed surprise. "I feel great."

"Aunt Emily says you've been working too hard and worrying far too much about that old hospital."

Her father raised a restraining hand. "Now just one moment, young lady! I'll not have you speaking of Benson Memorial Hospital in such a derogatory tone."

"I mean it, Dad," she insisted. "I think your health is worth a lot more than any forty-bed hospital."

Her father's face took on a grim look. "Don't blame the hospital," he said. "Blame the town council for wanting to shut it down."

"Whatever is wrong, I don't think you should let it bother you so."

"When you've put as many years of your life into something as I have into the Benson Memorial Hospital, it's difficult to let go and have others destroy it."

"Of course I understand that," she said. And then, with a small gesture of resignation: "But if it can't be prevented —"

"I'm by no means sure that it can't," her father said firmly.

Jane smiled. "I can see that I'll have to defer any discussion of this until you're in a better mood."

Her father stared at her for a long moment, the shrewd eyes under the shaggy white brows carefully appraising her. "Let's concentrate on you for a few minutes. I think you've lost weight since I saw you in Boston."

"You saw me such a short time I can't imagine that you noticed," she protested.

He looked wryly amused. "A professional habit. The minute I'm introduced to anyone, I begin diagnosing him."

"I've only lost a couple of pounds."

"Probably won't do you any harm," he said. "Most girls your age are starting to worry about putting on weight. How did you like working at the Peter Bent Brigham?"

"It's a wonderful hospital," she enthused. "They have the latest equipment and a fine medical staff."

He chuckled. "A bit more illustrious than the staff of the Benson Memorial, I'm afraid."

"But no more dedicated, I'm certain of that," Jane said.

"Thank you, my dear. We'll be glad to have you join us again. Miss McCumber was all aglow when I told her."

Jane hesitated, her pretty face clouding. She nervously clasped her hands in her lap. "I hadn't actually decided whether I'd stay on and nurse here," she said awkwardly. "I thought I'd come back and see how I adjusted first."

Her father's dignified features showed disappointment. "I understood from Emily you were definitely returning to the hospital."

Seeing how upset her announcement had made him, she quickly back-tracked. "I don't mind trying it for a week or two. What I meant is that I haven't made any definite decision about staying."

"All your friends will be glad to have you back," her father said seriously.

"I know that."

There was a moment of tactful silence before he asked, "You have gotten all over it, haven't you?"

Jane looked down at her hands. "I think so," she said in a small, dull voice. "I hope so. Now it all seems like a crazy dream."

"That's actually what it was," her father said with a sigh. "In your romantic dreams you saw Dick as the kind of person he never could be. And he used that easy charm of his to convince you that you were right." He paused. "I know I didn't help any by being so much against him. But I was terrified for you."

"It's all in the past now," she said in the same tone.

"But because of a single mistake, you mustn't assume you ruined your life," her father went on seriously. "I'm pleased that you are sad about the failure of your marriage. So many young people marry and divorce blithely today, ready and eager to make the same mistake again. You're not that sort of person, so this is more difficult for you. But you mustn't go to the other extreme. You have a wonderful life ahead of you, I'm sure."

She looked up at him gratefully. "Thank you, Father. I think I needed to hear you say those things."

His lined face showed his love for her. "I had to say them, since I fully believe I had a part in the failure. Now we must start to build again. And even though you met and married Dick here, there is no reason for you to feel ashamed to come back. People who saw Dick with clearer eyes than yours understand why your marriage failed."

Jane sighed. "But I have an awful feeling they'll be making comments behind my back."

"That will pass after a week or two at most," Graham Weaver said. "And I consider it most important that you come to terms with life in Whitebridge again. It will break your bondage to the unhappy past."

"I suppose it is the logical thing to do," she admitted.

"You haven't heard from Dick?" her father asked. "He hasn't bothered you?"

She shook her head. "No."

"I'm surprised."

"I'm not," she said. "He'd gotten himself into such a hopeless financial position after his drinking cost him his Florida job that he was terrified I'd demand alimony from him."

"I'm glad you didn't," her father said. "It was enough to be rid of him."

"I felt exactly the same way. But I'm sure it worried him. When he found out he wasn't going to have to pay anything, he just faded from the picture."

"Which is lucky for you. The man is worthless. You could have had no future with him." Her father sounded unusually stern.

At that moment Aunt Emily appeared in the doorway of the dining room with a smile on her plain face. "You two have talked long enough," she said. "I'm not going to have dinner spoiled by waiting."

Aunt Emily had lost none of her talent for cooking good plain meals. The steak dinner she'd provided for Jane's homecoming was an excellent example of her prowess in the kitchen. Jane sighed contentedly as she finished the apple dessert. It was good to be back.

At the head of the table, her father smiled. "Seems like the old days," he said.

"She just picked at her food," was Aunt Emily's lament. And she queried Jane, "Are you certain you won't have more dessert and coffee?"

"I couldn't, really!" Jane protested.

"I like to see people eat," her aunt said.

Jane's father chuckled. "I have to battle constantly to protect myself. I'd weigh two hundred and fifty pounds instead of a neat one hundred and seventy-two if she had her way."

Aunt Emily rose with a resigned look. "Well, don't say it isn't here to eat," she declared.

"I have to go back to the hospital for a half-hour," Jane's father announced. "Would you like to come along and see the new operating room?"

Jane showed interest. "I didn't know you had one."

Her father smiled. "It's a kind of patch-up job. But it's a big improvement over the old one. We have a new table, and it took some finagling to work that in on our limited budget. And the overhead lighting is of the most modern type. Some of the other equipment we had before."

"I'd like to go over and see it," she said, rising.

Graham Weaver got to his feet as well. "Again, it's going to seem pretty old-fashioned compared to what you've been used to in Boston."

She laughed. "You have a bad complex about Boston. They still use a lot of ancient equipment. They have to. It's too expensive to replace everything at once. And a lot of the time the men using the machines are as important as the machines themselves."

Her father's face brightened. "I can see you're developing a veteran's viewpoint," he commented.

They made the drive to the hospital in her father's car.

The hospital was on a side street off the tiny public square. It was a plain four-story brick building with iron fire escapes running down each side. The front entrance, like the rest of the building's architecture, was not impressive. It had been built for efficiency and economy. Yet the structure reflected a rock-like solidity.

Jane followed her father up the several granite steps to the entrance. He held the door open for her, and they mounted some inner steps to the lobby level.

Seated at a switchboard behind a counter in one corner of the lobby was Daisy Norris. Daisy was thirtyish and had pinched features and mouse-colored hair. In spite of a rather forlorn, stupid appearance, she was actually very bright and served as telephone operator, receptionist and head bookkeeper for the hospital.

Jane's father paused before the counter

as he told Jane, "You see our triple-threat girl is still here and doing a fine job."

"I'm sure she is." Jane smiled. "Hello, Daisy."

Daisy finished a call and jerked a plug from the switchboard. Turning to Jane, she removed her earphone for a moment. "Miss McCumber said you were coming, but I didn't expect you this soon," she said happily.

"I'm being given the grand tour," Jane said.

"You don't need one," Daisy assured her. "You know this place better than most of us. And it hasn't changed that much."

"Don't tell her that after I've spent all the dinner hour boasting about my operating room," Graham Weaver said.

The earphone began to make a screechy noise. Daisy sighed and clamped it to her ear. "I don't get a minute!" she complained. "And there are a few messages for you, Doctor."

"I'll check them as soon as I go to my office," he promised. And taking Jane by the elbow, he guided her to the self-service elevator.

When they were in the elevator, Jane said, "It's as though I'd left yesterday. Daisy never changes! She's wonderful!"

"I depend on her a good deal," her father said. "She is reliable, and that's especially important around a hospital."

They got off the elevator on the second floor, and Jane's father walked with her down the corridor leading to the main surgery room with a small scrub area next to it. He smiled at Jane as they reached the door to the operating room.

"Ready for the big surprise?" he wanted to know.

She was touched by the pride and pleasure he was showing in the room. It served to underline how much the hospital meant to him. She said, "Waiting with bated breath!"

"No need to drag out the torment." He laughed, opened the door and flicked a light switch.

Jane took in the new paint in a pale pastel green. She gave a small gasp of appreciation. "It's a lovely little room," she said.

Her father moved across to the shining stainless steel table with its many controls for bringing it into exactly the right position. He explained the several advantages of this particular table and why he'd chosen it.

Jane next gave her attention to the powerful overhead light. "You should be able to see with that," she declared.

"It's an excellent light," her father agreed. "Dr. Davis claims it is superior to any he's familiar with."

"I've met Dr. Davis," she said. "Maggie brought him around to the house for a minute."

Her father eyed her across the operating table, a knowing look on his face. "I guess she must have wanted you to meet him before you heard about him."

Her eyes questioned her parent. "He seems very nice."

"He's an excellent doctor and a fine human being."

"Has the friendship between him and Maggie caused any gossip?"

Her father offered her a tight smile. "Now what would your guess be?"

"That it has."

"And you're right," her father said, "but mostly among those with small minds and too much idle time. Sally Benson has gone on about it more than she has a right to."

Jane was plainly derisive. "Knowing Sally, I'm not surprised."

"She doesn't use any sense," Jane's father said with disgust. "I think her plan is to cover up her own actions by drawing attention to others."

"I know what you mean," Jane agreed. "What does Maggie's father think of it all?"

Dr. Graham Weaver shrugged. "Since he's the only druggist in town, 'most everyone drops into his store sometime. So he gets a fairly wide range of gossip. He snapped a couple of the worst offenders up, and I guess that was the end of it. He thinks Maggie is old enough to pick her friends wisely."

"And it is just a friendship?"

Her father looked at her with mild astonishment. "So far as I know," he said. "And it really is none of our business, is it?"

Jane blushed. "No. It isn't."

"Now let me show you the new instrument table," her father said, changing the subject and moving across the room. She accompanied him and listened as he went into the history of the table. When he finished he waved to the big clock with its sweeping second hand that dominated the wall over the entrance door. "That's a new clock, too. The old one wasn't large enough."

"I think you've done a fine job," Jane said, glancing around at everything again.

"Well, you've seen all that's new," her father said. "The rest of the place hasn't had any work. Nor is it likely to, with all this commotion about the council cutting off our funds."

She frowned as they started out. "They surely can't mean it."

"They mean it all right," her father mourned. "They aren't quite as close to medical practice as we are. They see things only in ledger figures. Lately the hospital has shown plenty of red ink." They emerged into the wide corridor as he flicked off the light and closed the door.

"You surely aren't overstaffed," Jane said.

"We're short of people in every department," her father said defensively as they strolled back to the elevator. "When I heard you were returning, I let Miss McCumber carry on for a fortnight without an assistant. We've had just the relief shift nurse and the practical who comes on at midnight."

Jane's eyebrows lifted. "You had more help than that before I left. You've really been pinching pennies."

"Not hard enough to please Mayor Benson and his councilmen."

"Is Steve really that difficult to deal

with?" she asked as they went down again in the elevator.

Her father's aristocratic face relaxed a trifle. "Steve is all right," he admitted. "It's that pack he has to deal with who cause all the trouble. They call themselves businessmen, and yet they can't see they're destroying one of Whitebridge's real assets if they close this place."

She could sympathize with her parent's point of view, but she supposed there was also another side to the matter. There were more than enough hospitals in the area in these days of rapid transportation.

When they left the elevator, he said, "If you'll excuse me a minute, I'll have to answer some of those calls. You can wait in my office or go up and visit the ward. We have a half-dozen patients. The relief nurse will be on duty."

Jane hesitated. "It's getting close to nine. She'll be busy with night medications. I won't bother her just now. Anyway, I'll be coming in for duty tomorrow, and I'll see them all then."

"Just as you say." Her father hesitated.

"You go on make your phone calls." She smiled. "I'll talk to Daisy in the lobby."

Her father nodded. "Very well." And he went away in the direction of his office.

Jane walked slowly along the corridor. She was wrapped in her thoughts when she collided with a tall, pleasant young man who had come hurrying down the corridor.

"Sorry," he apologized. "That was really stupid of me!"

She smiled ruefully. "It was my fault."

"Not at all," he said. "Have you been visiting a patient?"

"No."

"I'm sorry," he said. "I thought you might be Mrs. Mullin's daughter. She was expecting her in tonight. I'm her doctor, Wallace Milton."

"Of course!" Jane said, brightening. "My father mentioned you to me. I'm Jane Weaver."

It was the doctor's turn to show pleasure. He extended his hand. "Welcome back, Miss Weaver. I've heard a great many things about you."

"Oh!"

He was quick to show embarrassment. "I mean I've heard what a capable nurse you are."

"Thank you," she said.

He had fine features and piercing gray eyes; his dark hair was starting to gray attractively at the temples. And there was a hint of sadness about the slim man's face that reminded her he was the man with the neurotic wife.

He smiled apologetically. "You'll excuse me. I have to check on a patient and I have someone waiting for me. I'll see you when you report for duty."

"Yes, of course," she said as he hurried on.

Reaching the lobby, she saw someone standing at the counter in conversation with Daisy. As Jane approached, the girl turned, and Jane was startled to see the pretty, rather cold face of Sally Benson. So she was the one who was waiting for Dr. Milton.

CHAPTER THREE

Sally Benson was wearing a low-cut dress of some orange floral print material which had the look and styling of truly expensive clothing. She carried a shiny white pocketbook and had matching white shoes. The summer outfit enhanced her perfect tanned skin and made her look more attractive than she actually was.

As soon as she recognized Jane, she left the counter and came to greet her. With a carefully formed smile on her patrician face, she drawled, "Jane Weaver! I certainly didn't expect to see you back here."

Jane took a deep breath. "Whitebridge is a hard town to stay away from. I'm sure you've realized that." It was a shot at Sally, who had returned home to live after grandly taking off on a New York advertising career.

The glacial blonde lifted her chin. "I had no desire to come back," she said superciliously. "It was Mother's poor state of health that brought me; nothing else!"

Jane knew the answer to that. Sally's mother had been neurotic for years, although nothing too much was wrong with her. So Sally was using her mother's illness solely as an excuse.

Jane asked politely, "How is your mother?"

"Not well at all," Sally said. "Fortunately, Dr. Milton seems to have a flair for understanding Mother. She has confidence in him, and I think he's helping her."

It was an old story, but Jane pretended to believe it. "I'm so glad," she told the other girl.

"Something stupid happened to my carburetor," Sally continued in her exclusive girls' school drawl. "So I've left my car down at Bailey's to be repaired. Mr. Milton is going up to the house to visit Mother anyway, and he invited me to drive there with him."

Jane wasn't impressed. She knew Bailey's garage would have gladly driven the blonde girl home if she'd requested it. Sally was known to be highly resourceful when it came to tracking down a male.

Jane said, "I just met Dr. Milton in the corridor. Our first meeting. He's very handsome."

Sally didn't flick an eyelid. "I suppose he

would appeal to some girls," she said, as if the idea had never occurred to her.

"Too bad he is married," Jane said.

Sally's even features appeared more icy than they had before. "I've taken very little interest in his private life," she said.

It struck Jane that Daisy at the switchboard was probably overhearing a good deal of the conversation and enjoying it. She said, "I imagine I'll get to know him better when I come to work again."

"You're coming back to the hospital?" Sally asked sharply. "Then your marriage did turn out as badly as everyone predicted?"

Jane crimsoned. "I'm on my own again."

"How terrible for you!" Sally said cattily.

"Not really," Jane said. "I realize it's better this way."

"I'm sure you're right," Sally agreed airily. "I always say if you can't hold a man's love, why try to hold the man?"

Jane worked hard to restrain her anger. "It wasn't exactly like that," she said. "It is too complicated to discuss."

The other girl took her compact from the white pocketbook and set to work touching up her face. As she stared into the tiny mirror, she said, "I understand exactly how you must feel. But I don't think you should count on a career here in Whitebridge. You must have heard the hospital is soon to be shut down."

"I've heard some talk. It hasn't worried me."

"It should," Sally said, looking at her with smug hostility as she snapped the compact closed and thrust it in her pocketbook again. "I'm quite certain the town is fed up with paying out ridiculous sums merely to be able to say it has its own hospital."

"There's more to it than that," Jane said quietly. "The hospital offers the area a service it would be poorer without. They'll realize it if they do close it."

Sally smiled coldly. "But of course you'd be bound to take a different view from most of us. We feel the new hospital at Bladeworth is adequate for all our needs in these days of rapid transportation."

"It's a good argument," Jane admitted. "But I don't feel qualified to offer any final opinion."

"Naturally your father will always have his practice in Whitebridge," Sally went on in her patronizing way. "And at worst you could serve as a sort of receptionist for him."

"I had a very good nursing position at

the Peter Bent Brigham in Boston," Jane said. "They're eager for me to come back."

The blonde lifted her eyebrows ever so slightly. "I'd do that if I were in your shoes. You'll find things changed here. You remember my brother Steve. He's very interested in a girl in Dover. She was my best friend in college. I'm hoping they'll soon announce their engagement."

"I'm very happy for Steve," Jane said quickly.

"I'm sure you are," Sally agreed in her catty fashion. "After all, you two were fabulous friends for so long! But as I said, things do change."

Jane found herself both unwilling and unable to continue the barbed conversation with the girl. Sally was even more grimly overbearing than in the old days. The situation was saved by the sound of rapidly advancing footsteps coming down the corridor, and a moment later Dr. Wallace Milton made a smiling appearance.

"I'm sure you two know each other well," he said as he joined them. He stood between Jane and a smiling Sally.

"Of course," Sally said. "Jane lived here before her marriage."

Wallace Milton turned to her tactfully

and said, "I'm certain you'll be happy here again. The hospital needs you badly."

"I'm looking forward to working," Jane said. "I came up with Dad to see the improvements in the operating room."

The young doctor nodded. "He managed a lot with a woefully small budget. Dr. Weaver is a wonderful man!"

Sally quickly asked Jane, "Have you seen your friend Maggie Grant yet?"

"Just briefly," Jane said.

Sally smiled demurely. "She's been very busy. You'll be surprised to find she's developed a special interest in the medical profession, or at least in one member of it."

Dr. Wallace Milton gave the blonde girl a reproving glance. "I don't think you should say such things, Sally," he told her. And then a guilty look crossed his handsome face as he realized he had betrayed himself by using her first name. Confused, he said sharply, "We have to be getting on."

Sally apparently realized she had gone too far. She told Jane, "It's been divine seeing you again, darling!" and started out.

"Good evening, Miss Weaver," the young doctor said, and followed Sally to the door.

When they had both gone, she moved over to the counter where Daisy was seated with a look of disgust on her pinched face. The telephone operator put down her headphones for a moment.

"Hasn't changed a bit, has she?" Daisy asked.

"Not that I noticed."

"A little snip and always was!"

Jane smiled. "For some reason I seem to bring out the worst in her."

"That's because she knows her brother, Steve, has always been wild about you. She wouldn't want you as a sister-in-law! She'd rather play the heiress with you as the working girl. I know that one!"

"From what she says, Steve is about to get married."

"I wouldn't believe that!" Daisy said in disgust. "I've never seen him with any girl since you left."

"The girl lives in Dover."

"So she said! And I don't believe that either." The board lit up and buzzed. Daisy clamped on her earphones. "Excuse me a minute," she said as she went back to looking after the calls.

The activity at the telephone board ended, and Daisy put down the earphones and swung around to face Jane again.

"And did you hear the nasty reference to Maggie Grant and that nice Boyd Davis? She has a bad tongue in her head!"

"I was glad to hear Dr. Milton didn't approve."

"Not Dr. Milton," Daisy said. "There's nothing mean or miserable about him, though I guess the same can't be said for his wife."

Jane nodded. "I guess she's not too popular."

"Popular!" Daisy chortled. "The two or three times she's showed up in town she's insulted people."

"What's wrong with her?"

The telephone operator shook her head. "The way I was told, she has some kind of nervous trouble. She nags at the doctor every minute and thinks every time a female smiles his way it means a flirtation. I hear her jealousy has cost him most of his friends."

"That's too bad," Jane said, "since he seems so nice himself."

"It's always the way! Nice men get the worst women and vice versa!" was Daisy's bitter philosophy. "But she really has something to worry about this time. Sally is after the doctor."

"I wonder," Jane said. "He's attending her mother, you know."

Daisy dismissed this with scorn. "That's just Sally's excuse, part of her plan to trap poor Dr. Milton."

"He's probably intelligent enough to see through her."

The telephone operator pondered this dolefully. "I don't know," she said. "Did you hear him make that slip and call her Sally just now?"

"Yes."

"You see what I mean?" Daisy said with a knowing look on her pinched face. And then the telephone board came alive again to take her full attention.

Jane walked over to the other side of the lobby and sorted through some magazines which were scattered on a table there. She was flipping the pages of one when her father joined her. Dr. Graham Weaver looked apologetic.

"I'm sorry," he said. "I've kept you longer than I intended."

She smiled at him. "It didn't matter. I was in no hurry. I've been chatting with Daisy. And I met Dr. Milton."

"Yes, he was here to check on a patient," her father said. "What do you think of him?"

"He seemed very nice."

"Fine fellow and a competent doctor,"

he agreed warmly. "Still, I don't know whether we can hold onto him or not. He has some family problems."

"That's too bad."

Her father sighed. "That's always the story. It's desperately hard to get a good doctor to come to small towns today. Everyone wants to be a specialist." He glanced across at the telephone board. "I'll just give Daisy a few instructions and then we'll leave."

On the drive back home, he began to tell her of the case he and Dr. Milton were watching so carefully. "I did the actual operating," Dr. Weaver said, keeping his eyes on the street ahead. "Dr. Milton assisted, and Dr. Davis took over as anesthetist although that's usually Milton's job. But since it was his patient, I felt he ought to be involved directly in the operating."

Jane sat comfortably against the car seat in the semi-darkness and listened to her father's account of the operation. Surgery was the phase of medicine which interested him most.

"Milton's patient has cirrhosis of the liver," her father continued. "He has it so badly he could not hope to live for more than a few months without some miracle of medicine. We decided to gamble on a new type of procedure." He turned from the wheel a moment to glance at her. "You know what cirrhosis does to the liver?"

Jane nodded. "Yes. If I'm not mistaken, there is a replacement of the healthy liver tissue by dense fibrous tissue. This leads to an obstruction of the normal rate of blood through its substance for detoxification. As a result, all the body suffers."

"Exactly," her father said approvingly as he returned his attention to driving through the dusk-laden streets. "The new operation is called a porto-caval shunt and is accomplished by a suture of the portal vein to the vena cava. This detours the blood from the liver to the vena cava, and the load of work on the diseased organ is reduced. It usually permits a partial recovery of the cirrhotic liver. About half the patients are benefited."

"It sounds like a very difficult operation," Jane said.

"It was," her father agreed. "We had the patient on the table for close to six hours. But we pulled him through. Now it looks as if he may recover and regain his health. But we're watching him carefully for any signs of complications."

"I doubt if many doctors would try that operation."

She saw the smile that came to her father's aristocratic face. His profile was illuminated by the car's dash lights as he drove along. He said, "I didn't have much choice. The patient was going to die. I'd read up on the procedure. It went very well."

"I doubt if the Bladeworth clinic could have done better," she said.

"They have had a couple of similar cases," he admitted. "But only a few surgeons in this area would dare attempt the operation."

"If the man recovers it should be a good argument in favor of keeping the Benson Memorial alive."

"I think so," her father said dryly, "especially since the patient is Walter Milligan, the council member who has been most anxious to close us up."

"That's a coincidence."

"I find it an amusing one," her father agreed.

"But he can hardly fail to appreciate what the hospital means to Whitebridge if he recovers," Jane said.

"Well, I won't count on it," Dr. Graham Weaver said. "He's a mean old cuss. You can't be sure about him."

"But you feel reasonably sure the operation was a success?"

"I think so." Her father spoke with caution. "It will take a few more days before I'll be certain."

"Let's cross our fingers," she said.

They drove up into the yard. When Jane got out of the car, she was aware of the warm clear air of the night and the stars overhead. She had become so used to the smoke-laden air of the city that a night like this was a real treat.

She took a deep breath and walked slowly to the door of the screened porch, where her father stood waiting for her. Moths circled frantically in the glow of the single overhead light.

She smiled as she came up to her father. "On nights like this I can understand why you decided to spend your life in a small town."

Her father's lined face showed wistful amusement. "I'm perverse enough to like this White Mountain country in all seasons: the snowy peaks of winter, the running streams of spring, the lush beauty of our summers and the majesty of the autumn leaves in their crimson splendor."

Jane laughed as she went inside. "You should have been a poet, Dad."

"I was never cut out for that," he said as they entered the living room. Aunt Emily had left the lights on for them, and from her room upstairs there came the raucous sound of an action-filled television play.

Her father chuckled. "Emily has become more of a television fan than ever since you went to the city. She hates violence in real life, but she dotes on Westerns with plenty of gun play and hard-boiled mystery stories. I rarely see her in the late evenings." He settled himself on the end of the divan and began filling his pipe from a tobacco pouch he'd found in his jacket pocket.

Jane sat on the arm of a big easy chair across from him. Her lovely olive-skinned face showed concern. "But what about you? What do you do for pleasure or relaxation?"

Her father smiled and held up the straight-stemmed pipe. "My pipe," he said. "I allow myself the luxury of a rationed amount of tobacco."

"I wish you'd take it just a little easier," Jane worried. "You look so tired."

"That's age, not weariness," Dr. Graham Weaver assured her as he touched a match to his pipe and began to puff on it contentedly. "Things will be different now that you're back."

"I'd like to think so," Jane said. "Do you want me to report for the day shift tomorrow?"

59

Her father shook his head. Removing his pipe, he said, "You'll report for no shift tomorrow. I want you to have a day or two to rest before you start work."

"But I don't need it!" she protested.

"I disagree," he said. "You need that much time to become adjusted so you can give your full attention to your work when you do finally begin."

She gave him a rueful smile. "You treat me like a small girl or a not too bright patient."

"I want you to get a proper start," he said seriously. "And I think my advice is good."

"What will I do?" she demanded. "I'll be lost with nothing to do."

"Sleep late, read, have breakfast in bed," he said. "Do anything you like. Talk to old friends and take a stroll around the town."

"I do want to have a chat with Maggie Grant," she said. "I expect her to call me in the morning."

Her father nodded as he puffed on his pipe. "Ah, yes, Maggie," he said. He looked at her with shrewd eyes under shaggy white brows. "You and Maggie are close friends."

"She's my best friend."

Dr. Graham Weaver furrowed his brow.

"When you do talk to her, try to get some idea what she has in mind for the future. I don't mean that you should pry into her personal affairs, but try to see if there seems to be any change in her thinking."

Jane felt strangely on the defensive. She stared at her father. "You're wondering about her and Dr. Boyd Davis, aren't you?"

"Yes."

"Is that fair?"

"I think so," her father said mildly, taking his pipe from his mouth again as he deliberated on her question. "I'm not saying I'm opposed to my Negro colleague becoming romantically involved with Maggie. I'm merely worried for their sakes."

"It's none of our business."

"I disagree," her father said. "Boyd Davis is not only a fine doctor with the makings of a great one; he also has excellent training for the research field. I wouldn't like to have him faced with serious personal problems. His marriage to a white girl could easily disrupt his present way of life."

"I doubt if Maggie and he are thinking of marriage," Jane said. "But even if they were, it would be solely their concern."

"I applaud your liberal point of view," Dr. Graham Weaver said in his booming

61

voice. "I also am in favor of integration. But I'm doubtful if the town of White-bridge and the district of Rangely where Boyd Davis has his practice are as liberal-minded as we are."

"Then it's past time they were," she said.

"Granted," he agreed. "But that still does not change the realities of their situation for either Maggie or Dr. Davis."

"Maggie has always been level-headed," Jane countered.

"So were you until one day you told me of your plans to marry Dick," her father reminded her.

"That was different!"

"Now you're showing yourself to be partisan. There is nothing different in this from your own case. These people are just as apt to fall in love and be temporarily blinded to the odds stacked against them in a society that ignores or jeers a poor people's march on Washington. I'd like very much to know if they are in love. And if they are, I have an idea you might be the first to hear about it."

Jane was confused by her father's quiet words. She frowned. "Would you expect me to betray a confidence?"

"I'd count on you wanting to help Maggie and Dr. Davis."

"How would telling you of their plans help them?"

"I might be able to give them advice, help them through what would surely be a personal crisis," he said. "I was worried that Davis might not be accepted as the fine doctor he is in this area. Happily, he got off to a good start and proved himself. The people like him, and he's winning a local reputation. Marrying a town girl could wreck all that."

"Not if Dr. Davis is really accepted," Jane maintained firmly.

"Deep down, I'm not positive that he is in the sense we mean," her father said. "That is why I'm so worried."

"I see," she said quietly.

"I don't ask you to be disloyal," her father insisted. "I don't want you to question Maggie on the subject. But if she voluntarily tells you of any plans she and Boyd Davis may have, I'd like you to let me know about them."

CHAPTER FOUR

The next morning Jane slept late, had breakfast, then decided to follow her father's advice and take a walk around the small town.

The streets were almost empty of people. She did pass some houses where she saw neighbors in the yards or gardens and waved to them. Old Mr. Woodley was rocking in his chair in his screened porch just as he had done mornings for as long as she could remember. She waved to him and he waved back, probably without recognizing her. He was well over eighty and slightly vague.

At the junction with the main street, she encountered a family group of tourists on a sight-seeing and shopping expedition. The children ran ahead of their parents, who occasionally shouted warnings or commands to them. She turned down the main street and headed for the small square.

The triangle of green grass which Whitebridge had glorified with the name of square seemed strangely tiny to her now.

She waited for the traffic lights to change and then crossed to the block where Grant's Drugstore was located. In spite of its glossy new front and modern neon sign, it was a place of memories for her. When she swung the new aluminum-framed glass door open and entered the store, she found little that was familiar.

She stood for a moment surveying the new self-service counters and the cashier's station at the exit to total purchases and take payment. Gone was the familiar marble soda fountain with the old-fashioned silver fixtures. In its place was a circular coffee bar in the rear with stools all around it. And she saw that even at this early morning hour the bar was doing a good business. Tourists and local young businessmen filled most of the stools.

With a sigh she went on to inspect the shelves of the impersonal modern store which had replaced the friendly emporium she'd enjoyed only a few years ago. She was casually inspecting a counter devoted to souvenir ash trays and other tourist gift novelties when she heard a step behind her and turned to see Maggie's father standing there with a smile.

He was wearing a neat white smock, and though his thin face looked older, he seemed to have lost none of his good humor. "Little Jane Weaver," he said. "I've been hoping you'd drop by ever since your father told me you were back."

She smiled at him. "You're looking well, Mr. Grant."

The druggist smoothed a hand over his bald pate. "Aside from growing up through my hair, I'm as good as new." This was a favorite joke of his, she remembered.

Gesturing with her hand, she said, "I'm impressed by your new store. So different! So modern!"

He nodded without much enthusiasm. "The new drugstore," he said. "We carry everything from liver salts to sport clothes. The trend almost put me out of business. I didn't know how to stock a store like this. So I got wise and sold out to a chain. Now the only old-fashioned thing in here now is me. Part of the deal was that I stay on as manager."

Jane laughed. "I'm sure they were smart to insist on that."

The tall, bald druggist shrugged. "One of these days I'll slide out of this smock and take a good long rest. Your dad tells me you're going to be at Benson Memorial again."

"I guess so."

"They need you," Maggie's father said. "Nellie McCumber was in here the other night wailing about how short-staffed they are over there."

"With the hospital budget cut so much, I don't think Dad has any choice," Jane said.

Grant's long face became bleak. "If the council have their way, we won't have a hospital. And I don't dare say too much, or they'll claim it's because I want the extra drug business a hospital brings. And that's nonsense!"

"I know Dad is worried," she agreed.

"We all have our worries these days," the druggist said. Giving her a knowing look, he went on, "You've seen Maggie, haven't you?"

"I have, and I'm hoping we can get together tonight."

He nodded. "It will be good for her to have you here again. She's at a time in her life when she has to make an important decision. I'm hoping she makes the right one."

"Of course," Jane said, feeling uncomfortable.

"I don't want to interfere," the druggist went on. "I'm in no position to know to advise her. I only want her to be happy."

"I know you do."

Grant smiled again. "Well, life is never easy, is it? And it wouldn't be much fun if it was. We have to be able and willing to accept challenges as they come along."

Jane gave a small sigh. "You're so right. I've been an awful coward about coming back here. I've felt sure I'd be gossiped about."

"You have a lot of friends in White-bridge," Maggie's father said. "So don't you worry."

"I'm beginning to feel a little easier," she admitted. "But I still don't think it would take much to send me scurrying."

"Your dad needs you here."

"That's what Aunt Emily says."

"And she's right," Grant went on seriously. "I've seen him age in the last few months. I can't understand how the town can treat him this way after all he's done for it."

"I'm sure Dad doesn't expect any special respect or gratitude," she said. "But I do know he believes we need the hospital."

"I realize that," the druggist agreed. "But sometimes I wonder. I see what the years have done to my small business, and I realize there have been changes that make it less urgent we have a hospital here today than when Benson donated the money for it."

Jane was worried by what he had said. She knew there was a lot of truth in it.

"I hope it's soon settled," she said. "Whichever way it goes, I'm sure he'd be a lot easier in his mind once he knew what was going to happen."

"I don't blame him for fighting for the hospital," the druggist said. "He believes he's right, and maybe he is."

"It's been good talking with you, Mr. Grant," she said. "Be sure and tell Maggie to call me."

"I will," the druggist said as he strolled with her to the door.

Only when she stepped out into the warm morning sunshine again did Jane realize that the drugstore was air-conditioned now, along with all the other improvements. As she strolled along toward the end of the block, she considered what the druggist had said.

She was deep in her thoughts when a car horn blared almost beside her. It gave her a shock, and she halted and stared in the direction from which the sound had come. Seated in a gray convertible with its top down was Steve Benson!

"Steve!" she gasped. "You almost frightened me to death."

"The last thing I'd ever want to do," he

assured her with a smile as he leaned over to open the door for her to enter. "Come on; we'll go for a drive."

She hesitated at the curb. "I shouldn't. I planned to go back to the house. I only got here yesterday."

"I know," he said. "And I've been wanting to see you ever since I heard you were back. We'll go as far as the river and back. It won't take more than a half-hour. We have things to talk about." This last was said seriously.

Jane smiled at him. In his fawn summer suit and neat brown-striped tie, he looked the immaculate young businessman he was. His curly brown hair with its part on the left was ruffled by the wind, and his tanned, lean face as good-looking as ever.

She said, "All right," and got in beside him.

Steve expertly guided the car down a side street and along a short narrow block, and came out on the road leading to the main highway and the river. As they reached the main road, he gave her a brief glance.

"You're looking great," he said.

Jane enjoyed the compliment. "So are you."

His eyes were on the heavily traveled

highway as he went on to ask, "What made you decide to come back?"

"My father. He isn't too well."

"I know," Steve said. "The hospital thing. I'm sorry about it. I've had to take sides against him as mayor. But I've still fought for him to have a fair chance to present his arguments."

"I'm sure you have," she said. There was quiet resignation in her tone.

He glanced at her again. "You know Benson Memorial's days are probably numbered?"

"It's too bad. Father thinks it should be kept operating."

"I doubt if the council will grant him any more money," Steve warned. "The September budget will decide the issue. The hospital can't manage on the trust fund money alone."

"That's the main reason I've come back," she said. "I feel I ought to be here when all this is settled."

"You're going to work at the hospital?"

"Yes."

"I'm glad of that," he said with a smile. "For purely selfish reasons, of course. I was afraid you might be here for just a few days."

They were well out of town now, and the

71

view of the surrounding mountains was most impressive. The winding road had turnout spots at various points to allow cars to park and the occupants to enjoy the bluegray peaks with their growth of evergreens. She knew that Steve was driving to one of these parking places which overlooked a swift, narrow river. It had once been a favorite spot of theirs.

"I saw Sally at the hospital last night," she said.

"Oh?" He seemed surprised. "Sis didn't mention it. The service station man at your corner told me you were back."

"She probably forgot about it," Jane said. "She was with Dr. Milton. They were on their way to see your mother. Sally was quite concerned."

Steve took his eyes away from the wheel a moment to give her an odd look. "You must be kidding! Mother is away visiting her brother."

Jane was flustered.

She quickly said, "I'm sure I must have misunderstood her."

Steve's strong profile was grim as he watched the road ahead. "I doubt it. You know she's got a crazy crush on Wallace Milton, and she's using any excuse to see him."

"I haven't been back long enough to hear any gossip," she said.

"Well, you'll hear about it soon enough," Steve assured her. "She's causing plenty of talk around town. Mother's upset and so am I. Milton is a nice fellow, and he has a wife who's not any help to him."

"So I've heard."

"Sally is bound to cause bad trouble if she keeps on acting the way she has been," was Steve's comment. "I've given up on her."

They had come to the turnout by the river, and he wheeled the car over to the parking area. Happily, it was deserted at the moment. He got out, came around and opened the car door for Jane.

"Let's stroll down to the observation platform," he suggested.

She smiled as she joined him. "I think the last time we were here was after one of the club dances. A grand night! There were stars and a moon that made the mountain peaks glisten like blue diamonds."

Steve regarded her affectionately. "I haven't your gift for poetry," he said. "But I do remember the night."

The path to the observation platform took them below the level of the parking place and highway. There were rough

73

stone steps at some points along it, and the platform itself was built of logs with a rough plank floor and a shingled roof to serve as a shade and protection against the weather. From the railing of the platform they could plainly hear the water as it rushed down a rocky formation to make a picturesque waterfall.

Jane stared down at the foam-flecked water racing over the rocks about thirty feet below. "It's lovely," she said. "And its sound shuts out all the traffic noise."

"It's a refuge," Steve agreed. "Once in a while I come here alone. It's a good place to think."

She shifted her gaze to his serious, lean young face. "It's good to see you again, Steve. I hope things have been going well for you."

He spread his hands. "I've kept busy. I took on the mayor's job at a time when there are plenty of headaches. And we've had some labor troubles at the plant."

"They seem to have them everywhere."

Steve's eyes met hers. "A lot of the time I've wondered and worried about you."

"You shouldn't have."

"I had no choice. I knew you'd never be able to stay married to Dick. I think I knew him as well as anyone in Whitebridge. It

74

just couldn't work out. So I wasn't surprised when I heard about the divorce. But I was worried that you didn't come back."

She leaned on the rail and watched the water tumbling over the rocks. "I made such a stupid mistake," she said. "My pride wouldn't let me come back."

"You shouldn't have felt that way. I know you thought you were in love with Dick and that you felt you understood him. No one could blame you because he let you down."

"People aren't all as generous as you," she said bitterly. "Sally wasn't when I talked with her last night."

"Sally is a little fool," Steve told her. "She's also mean and barb-tongued. You mustn't pay any attention to her."

"Some of what she said was the truth," Jane admitted. "I suppose I have to expect to suffer for my stupidity."

Steve's arm went around her. "That's over with," he said in a quiet voice. "It's your future that's important."

She nodded. "I'll stay until the hospital business is settled. Then I'll probably leave again."

His arm tightened around her. "Even if I ask you to stay?"

Jane looked up into his handsome face.

"Don't pretend," she said. "We've both changed. I know it's too late for us."

"You couldn't be more wrong!"

"Please, Steve!" She looked away again. "I know you've been seeing someone in Dover."

"In Dover?" He sounded bewildered.

"It's not important!"

"I think it is," he persisted. "In Dover?" he repeated. And then, as if a sudden light had come to him, he asked, "You don't mean Ruth Hennessey?"

"Please, Steve!" she begged. "I don't want to talk about it."

"But I do," he said, his arm still around her. "Ruth is the sister of a college friend of mine. She's running her father's business in Dover and had tax problems. I went over a few times to help her straighten them out. That's all there was to it."

"I heard you're about to announce your engagement."

"Then you heard wrong," Steve said. And he turned her toward him and pressed his lips to hers. For just a moment she forgot the problems that beset them and was comforted by the gentle refuge of his arms.

Their moment of bliss was ended by the

sound of voices coming down the path above them. A child's gleeful cry caused them to part quickly as a family of tourists descended on the platform.

Steve smiled at her wryly. "I guess it's time for us to go."

She nodded and quickly touched her hankie to his lips to remove any traces of her lipstick.

Steve helped her up the steep path and saw her safely in the car again. As he slid behind the wheel, he gave her a warm smile. "We'll have to continue our talk sometime soon."

She gave him a warning glance. "Steve, you mustn't think it's all settled, that we can start over just where we broke off two years ago. I can't promise that. I have to have more time to think, more time to see how I'm accepted in town."

"I'm in love with you," he said. "I always have been. What else matters?"

"A lot," she said. "I'm not going into it now. We should be getting back to town. We've been gone more than the half-hour you promised."

He smiled wryly. "I don't think the time has been wasted. And I can see I'm going to have to use a lot more persuasion with you."

She said nothing but settled back against the convertible's leather seat as he started the engine and headed the car back onto the road.

"You're very quiet," he said.

"You've given me something to think about," she replied with a rueful smile.

"Stay away from all that thinking," was his advice. "Let me do the planning for us."

"We'll see," she said vaguely.

"And keep away from Sally," he warned her. "Don't pay any attention to what she says."

They talked little during the rest of the drive into town. And when he drove up before her father's big slate green house, she quickly opened the car door to get out.

Steve put a hand on her arm to hold her back. "I'll expect to see you soon again," he said with an earnest expression on his lean young face.

"After I get properly settled and back at the hospital," she told him.

"I'm the impatient type," he said. "Let me decide when it will be."

"Please, Steve," she begged, "let's not repeat any mistakes."

His handsome face was somber. "I hadn't expected we would."

She managed a wan smile. "I'll see you after a little." And she left the car and closed the door.

Steve stared at her. "Don't forget what I told you," he said. And with a final wave he drove off.

She turned and slowly made her way to the side door and into the house. Aunt Emily was waiting for her in the living room. And at once she sensed something unusual in the big woman's manner.

Aunt Emily said, "You were gone longer than you expected."

"Yes, I met Steve. We went for a drive."

"Oh." The big woman's plain face wore a wise expression. "You have company."

Jane frowned. "Company? I wasn't expecting anyone."

"I had her wait in your father's office," Aunt Emily said. "I thought you might have more privacy there. She's been waiting quite awhile. I'd go see her at once if I were you."

Jane gave her aunt a puzzled glance and then went quickly down the shadowy hall to her father's office. The door was open, and she went inside to find a middle-aged Negro woman seated in one of the easy chairs.

The woman got up at once and said, "Miss Warren, I'm Boyd Davis' mother."

79

CHAPTER FIVE

Jane managed to control her surprise. She mustered a small smile of greeting as she said, "I'm happy to know you, Mrs. Davis." She closed the door after her so they wouldn't be overheard.

"I apologize for intruding on you Miss Weaver," the older woman said. "But I understand you are a close friend of Miss Grant's, and I hope you will forgive me." Her voice had a pleasant lilting quality.

"It's all right, Mrs. Davis," Jane said. She indicated the chair and suggested, "Please sit down."

Mrs. Davis seated herself. Jane could see the resemblance between mother and son, although Mrs. Davis had a lighter skin coloring than Boyd. She had a great deal of character in her face, and while she could never have been a beauty, she had a nice cast of features. She was dressed tastefully in a yellow linen dress with matching accessories. Her hair was graying and had little curl.

Mrs. Davis said, "I'm a newcomer to the area, so we haven't met before. I came here a year ago to keep house for my son."

Jane was seated opposite her. "I have met your son," she said. "He seems very nice."

Mrs. Davis sat primly in the easy chair. "Boyd is a fine man and an excellent doctor," she said.

"I have heard him praised on all sides."

The Negro woman gave her a knowing look. "I'm proud that he has won a place for himself here. And I'm very anxious that he shouldn't lose it."

Jane nodded. "I can understand that."

Mrs. Davis hesitated for a moment before she asked, "Have you any idea of the danger there is of that? I mean because of his friendship with Miss Grant."

Jane made a frustrated gesture with her right hand. "I've only just come home. I haven't had a chance to talk with Maggie."

"In a way I'm glad of that," the older woman said with a troubled expression on her pleasant face. "This gives me a chance to offer my opinion of her friendship with my son before you see her. And perhaps you can make her understand my feelings in the matter."

Jane said, "I'd hesitate to offer any opinions."

81

Mrs. Davis gave her a direct look. "I'm assuming Miss Grant will ask for your advice. Since you are her best friend, it seems a reasonable assumption."

"She probably will bring the subject up," Jane admitted. "But then again she may not, since she knows I have several problems of my own."

The woman across from her nodded. "I've come to you just on the chance that she may ask your opinion about marrying my son."

"I understand."

"Their friendship has caused a certain amount of gossip," the older woman went on. "But so far no real harm has been done. I've asked my son what his intentions are, and he insists he and Miss Grant are merely good friends. But I don't think such a close friendship between a man and woman can continue without becoming more serious."

Jane was impressed by the woman's cool consideration of the problem and the careful way in which she was expressing herself. She said, "You may be allowing yourself to become concerned without any reason. Maggie is a serious intellectual type, and I'd judge your son is also a very responsible sort of man. A platonic friendship between two such people can be a deep and rewarding thing."

"I've tried to tell myself that," Mrs. Davis said. "And perhaps it is true. But I know that Boyd is vulnerable because he is such a lonely person. His success has shut him off from our family and his friends of younger days. He has only me. And I'm obviously not enough."

Jane smiled. "I think he is fortunate to have a mother like you. You surely must have played a big role in making Boyd what he is today."

Mrs. Davis sighed. "I have always been an ambitious person, Miss Weaver, and I suppose my son is the end product of my ambitions. In my generation, the role of the Negro in the United States was pretty clearly defined. I was a domestic. An exalted one with a special position in the household of a wealthy and considerate family, but I was still a domestic."

"I understand," Jane said.

"My late husband was a postal clerk," the older woman went on. "I think had his skin been white, he would have held an executive position. He had a fine mind. He did his work well and was a success in his modest way. He and I did not have to face the problems Boyd faces today. Integration wasn't a familiar word then."

"I'm sure Boyd is equal to any situation," Jane said seriously.

"I think he is a mature person," his mother agreed. "And I assume Miss Grant is a fine, intelligent girl. But what they don't recognize is that the attitude of this community, many communities, has not reached their level of understanding. I'm afraid both my son and Miss Grant would be badly hurt if they decided to marry."

Jane frowned. "How can you be so sure?"

"A result of experience," Mrs. Davis said firmly. "Doors would be closed to Boyd that are open to him now. Chances to further his career would be lost. I think Miss Grant would suffer in other ways. And if she does love my son, it would hurt her to realize she had ruined his career."

"I still say you're taking it for granted he will be hurt. I'm not sure that is so. There are quite a number of mixed marriages among people of some prominence today. I can't say that it has harmed any of them."

"You have confidence because your skin is white," Mrs. Davis said calmly. "I worry because I am a Negro mother. I'm selfishly concerned for my son and his future. Nothing else matters."

"I sympathize with your position," Jane assured her.

"Boyd and I do not represent the Negro race any more than you and your father represent the white one," Mrs. Davis said. "We are individuals, and we understand each other. But most of the time, when racial matters are discussed, whole groups are taken as stereotypes. The black man becomes tagged as lazy, uneducated and a relief agitator, and the white is dubbed superior, responsible and tolerant. Neither these pictures nor their opposites are true, and so we have a wide gulf of confusion between our races. That's the chasm my son and Miss Grant would find a fatal trap."

"Why don't you make it a point to see Miss Grant and tell her exactly how you feel?" Jane suggested.

The older woman shook her head. "I have a strange sort of pride, Miss Weaver. Boyd has not chosen to do more than introduce me to her. I do not want to find myself begging her for my son's future. But I did feel I could explain the danger as I see it to you, and perhaps you might be able to convince her marrying Boyd would be wrong for both of them."

Jane looked down at her folded hands. "I

won't try to convince her of anything. But I will point out what you have made so clear. And I'll let her know how you feel if she should ask me."

"That's fair," Mrs. Davis said quietly, and stood up. "Again I apologize for troubling you."

Jane got to her feet with a smile. "I'm pleased to have had this chance to meet you. We must see each other again."

"I don't often leave our house in Rangely," Mrs. Davis said. "I have a nice vegetable and flower garden. It takes a great deal of time."

Jane saw the woman out the front door, since it was the most convenient. As they emerged in the sunlight of the front steps, she asked, "Do you have a car?"

"No," the older woman said. "Boyd drove me down when he came to the hospital this morning. I sometimes come to Whitebridge for shopping and take the afternoon bus back."

"But that doesn't leave for nearly an hour, unless the schedule has been changed," Jane said. "Why not let me drive you home?"

Mrs. Davis smiled her gratitude. "No thanks," she said firmly. "I prefer to take the bus."

Jane remained on the steps to watch the lonely figure of the proud, defiant Negro woman as she walked down the street, then returned to the living room. Aunt Emily was seated there in an easy chair, busy with her knitting needles and the beginnings of a red sweater.

She raised her eyes as Jane entered and asked, "Has Mrs. Davis gone?"

"Yes," she said. "I let her out the front way."

"Her son looks a lot like her."

"I noticed that," Jane said, going over to the window and staring out at the yard and her car under the shade of the big elm.

"Did you have a nice talk?" Aunt Emily wanted to know.

"It was revealing," Jane told her, still staring out of the window. "I think she's a fine person."

"No doubt," her aunt said dryly.

Jane could tell the older woman was curious about the Negro woman's call. But she did not feel it proper to betray the confidence Mrs. Davis had shown in her, so she kept silent on the subject. Aunt Emily might feel mildly hurt, but it had to be that way.

"Whom did you see when you were in town?" her aunt wanted to know.

87

Jane welcomed the change of subject. She said, "I stopped by the drugstore and saw Mr. Grant for a few minutes. And then I happened to meet Steve Benson."

"Mayor Benson," her aunt said wisely. "I'll bet he was glad to see you."

Jane turned to her. "We had a nice talk."

Aunt Emily looked up from her knitting needles, disdain showing on her plain face. "Did you tell him to stop the council from nagging your father about the hospital?"

"I could hardly do that," Jane said with a wry smile. "But he did bring the matter up. It seemed to me he isn't too hopeful."

"I know it," Aunt Emily said. "They've made up their minds to withdraw their support of Benson Memorial. I've tried to prepare your father for it, but he refuses to listen."

"Perhaps he feels they may still change their minds."

"They won't."

Jane sighed. "I don't think I can adjust to sitting around. I'm going to ask Dad if I can start day duty at the hospital to-morrow."

"He wants you to have a good rest."

"I don't need one," she argued. "I'd be a lot better off working."

"Then tell him so," Aunt Emily said.

"He seems to pay some attention to what you say. He won't listen to me at all."

"I'm sure he does," Jane said with a small laugh. "You just have that idea."

"It's the truth," Aunt Emily said. "Graham tolerates me as a housekeeper, and that's all. I wish I'd had the good sense to find myself a husband when I was your age."

Jane paid no attention to this. It was a familiar lament on her aunt's part and one which she didn't feel had much meaning. She had always known her aunt to enjoy her independence, and she couldn't picture her as being happy in marriage. Aunt Emily had her various clubs and activities and lived a pleasant, busy existence.

Jane went upstairs to her room and changed into a pair of white shorts and a brown paisley shirt which had an open neck. She donned dark sun glasses and found herself a book. Then she went down to the front lawn and settled in one of the several metal chairs her father had set out there. She soon got lost in the novel and didn't hear her father's car when it came into the yard.

"Well, you seem to be enjoying your leisure," he said in his hearty tone as he came to stand by her. He was bareheaded to the sun, wearing a light gray suit and carrying his medical bag in his hand.

Jane looked up from her book with a smile. "It is a good book, but I'm getting restless. I want to start work in the morning."

Her father's white eyebrows raised. "Are you sure?"

"Very sure."

"All right, then," he said. "Miss McCumber will be glad to have you. The summer rush of visitors has raised our bed count. We had twenty-one patients this morning. That's a record for the year."

She smiled. "You see, I've been back only a day, and already the tide is turning."

He shook his head with a grim smile. "I'm afraid when the summer season is over, the tide will go out permanently."

"Don't be too sure," she said, although she knew he was probably right. "Are you home to begin office hours?"

Her father nodded. "Yes. My first patient is due any minute." And he left her to go inside.

Jane buried her head in the novel again and was thoroughly absorbed in the story when she heard someone coming over to her. Looking up, she was surprised to see the handsome Dr. Wallace Milton.

He smiled uneasily. "Good afternoon, Miss Weaver. We meet again."

She returned his smile. "Yes. Are you looking for Dad? He has a waiting room full of patients."

"Not really," he said. "I'm trying to locate my wife. You don't know if she's in there, do you? She spoke of coming to see your father the other day."

"I'm afraid I wouldn't know her."

"Of course not; I'd forgotten," he said. "She's a little older than you and taller. Has about your shade of hair?"

"I've not been watching closely," she said. "I really couldn't say whether she's in there or not."

Dr. Milton glanced toward the house with a frown. "She left home this morning," he said. "And she hasn't been back since. The housekeeper was worried about her and got in touch with me."

"You had better check inside then," Jane suggested.

He glanced at her absently. "Yes, I will do that," he said. "Sorry to have interrupted your reading."

"That doesn't matter," she said.

He left her and strode across to the front door, a tall, athletic figure in his fawn summer suit. No wonder, she thought,

Sally Benson had a crush on him. He was surely a romantic type.

It was only a few minutes before he quickly came out again. He walked over to her and, with an awkward smile, said, "She wasn't in there. I called my home again, and she's just returned. She went for a hike in the woods."

"You must be glad to know that," Jane said, shading her eyes against the strong rays of the sun.

"I am," he said with a small sigh. "She hasn't been too well lately. I worry about her."

"That's too bad."

He continued to linger there. "You're a good friend of Sally's," he said at last.

She said, "Not really. I know her brother better."

"Steve," the young doctor said, "is a fine fellow. He's made a good mayor, though, being part of the hospital, I can't agree with his views on Benson Memorial."

"I'm sure he's merely expressing the entire council's opinion," she said.

"No doubt about that. They're after our scalps," Wallace Milton said with a thin smile. "You must meet my wife one of these days."

"I'd like that," Jane told him.

"I'll have Ruth call you," he said. "She used to enjoy arranging small dinner parties. I'm going to try to get her interested again." With a final smile he went to his car and drove away.

Jane continued to sit out on the lawn as the patients gradually left. She was sitting there when she heard her Aunt Emily calling her from the side porch. Getting up quickly, she went to the side door.

"Maggie is on the phone," Aunt Emily said. "She wants to speak to you."

"Thanks," Jane said, and hurried inside to take the call at the hall extension. Picking up the phone, she spoke into the receiver. "Sorry to keep you waiting, Maggie. I was sitting on the front lawn."

"And a good afternoon for it," Maggie said. "I've called to ask if you'd have dinner at the country club with me."

"What time?" Jane asked. "I'll have to dress."

"There's no hurry," Maggie told her. "How about in an hour? I'll reserve a table on the porch. I like to watch them golf. Gives me a chance to enjoy the game without having to exercise."

"Sounds wonderful," Jane responded.

"I'll pick you up in my car," Maggie suggested. "You haven't any plans for later in the evening, have you?"

"No."

"Fine," Maggie said. "That will give us a leisurely period to talk. I've been looking forward to it."

"So have I," Jane said. "I'll be expecting you in an hour."

She told Aunt Emily she'd be having dinner out and then went upstairs to take a shower and dress. The Whitebridge Country Club was the scene of most of the social activity in the small town. Its golf course was its chief feature, but there were also Saturday night dances, and the club dining room served meals all through the golfing season. There had been rumors the club would be made an all-year-round one when skiing activity was introduced for the winter months. But so far nothing had been done about this.

Jane had not kept her membership in the club, although her father still had his.

By the time she'd changed to a dark dress with a low back and high ruffled neck line, almost the whole hour had gone by. She carefully selected a silver pin to decorate the dress and placed it directly below the neck. Satisfied, she hurriedly picked up her black handbag and went downstairs.

She met her father in the living room. He smiled at her indulgently. "You're looking very smart tonight," he said, studying her dress. "Emily tells me you're having dinner at the club with Maggie."

Jane nodded. "She called me a little while ago."

"Have a good time," he said.

"I will," she promised. "She's picking me up in her car."

"By the way," her father said. "Are you sure you want to begin work in the morning?"

"I definitely do," she assured him.

"I'll let Miss McCumber know," he said.

"Did you see Dr. Milton when he was here?" she asked.

Her father looked surprised. "No. When was that?"

"Late this afternoon. He was looking for his wife. He must just have checked your waiting room, and when he didn't see her there he phoned his house. She'd shown up by that time."

Her father frowned. "I don't like the sound of that. They may be having trouble again."

"He seemed nervous," she said.

"I must give him a phone call later," her father said. "I'm glad you mentioned it."

Their talk was brought to an end by Maggie signaling her arrival with two mild blasts of her horn. Jane kissed her father on the cheek and ran out to join her friend.

Maggie had the door open for her and sat behind the wheel, looking extremely attractive in a pale blue outfit that flattered her blondeness. She said, "You certainly didn't keep me waiting."

Jane slid in beside her. "I've been ready for a few minutes. I was just talking to Dad." She closed the car door.

Maggie headed the car out into traffic. "It's such a fine night I thought this might be fun."

"I'm glad you suggested it," Jane said.

"Adjusting to our town again?"

"I think so. There have been a few pains, but minor ones."

"I didn't know how you'd feel about the club, since Dick was the pro there when you met," Maggie said frankly. "But I didn't think it would do any harm to suggest going there."

"I don't mind," Jane told her. "I have to get used to facing memories if I'm going to stay here."

Maggie swung the car into the street that led to the main highway and the country club. "I'd call that sensible thinking. It will be nice to have a meal at the club. I haven't been there much lately."

"I suppose not," Jane said. Since the Whitebridge Country Club was a staid private club, it followed that Dr. Boyd Davis would not be welcome there.

CHAPTER SIX

The Whitebridge Country Club was a sprawling colonial style white building with a number of additional wings which had been added over the years. It was located on a side road on a small rise with the golfing area directly in back of it. The table Maggie had reserved on the porch overlooked the links.

Henry, the white-haired Italian who came up from Boston each summer to serve as headwaiter, showed them to the table and beamed as he handed them menus.

"It has been too long since you girls were here," he said warmly.

"We're glad to see you're still here, Henry," Maggie said with a smile.

He raised a hand. "I go with the lease, Miss Grant. Have a good dinner, both of you." And he signaled a waiter as he left them.

They ordered and then sat back to relax. There were a number of golfers still playing, and they watched them for a few minutes, enjoying the contrast of the smooth greens with the blue mountaintops in the background.

Maggie studied Jane across the table. "How does it feel to be back?" she asked.

Jane smiled. "Not as bad as I thought it would."

"I'm glad you decided to come. I've been lost without you."

"I want to begin working," Jane said. "I do better when I'm busy. Dad has promised I can start in the morning."

"I was going to summer school," Maggie said. "Then at the last minute I changed my mind."

"No doubt you have plenty to do at home," Jane said.

"I have," her friend agreed. "The only time I can catch up on housecleaning is in the summer. Dad scolds me for staying in and working. But it has to be done. Once school begins, there just isn't any time."

Their food came, and it was excellent. They said little during the dinner, waiting until they were lingering over coffee to resume their conversation.

Maggie began by saying, "I suppose you've met Wallace Milton."

"Yes. Several times. He's very handsome."

Her friend smiled grimly. "Sally Benson thinks so."

"I understand that."

"I wouldn't bring it up," Maggie went on, "except that she's been very busy spreading malicious gossip about Boyd Davis and me."

Jane shrugged. "You know what Sally has always been like."

"She's worse now," Maggie said with a slight frown. "I couldn't believe she was deliberately trying to hurt Boyd and me at first. I doubted what people told me she was saying. And then at a cocktail party one of the summer people gave, I happened to overhear her myself. It was so hateful I cringed."

Jane stirred her coffee deliberately. "I'm sure most people have Sally measured for the sort of person she is. Don't you think it would be best to ignore her talk?"

"It would be easy for me," her friend agreed. "But other people do listen to her. And some of the people here don't know her well enough to discount what she says."

"That's too bad."

The blonde Maggie's pretty face was a study in frustration. "I've even spoken to Steve about her. But he says it's impossible to do anything with her."

Jane nodded. "He never was able to reason with Sally. She's always been stubborn and spoiled."

"Now she's downright impossible," Maggie declared. "I believe she is crazy about Dr. Milton. She knows there is gossip about them, and so she spreads this rubbish about Boyd and me to try to divert people's attention."

"I don't think she's been too successful," Jane pointed out. "There is trouble between Dr. Milton and his wife. I know, because he came to our place looking for her today. She'd gone away without leaving word, and he seemed badly worried."

Maggie showed interest. "I know they don't get along well. She's wildly jealous of him. And it's likely someone has told her about Sally, even if they haven't named her."

"As I hear it, Wallace Milton is a very decent sort," Jane said. "And he's trying to get rid of Sally and her unwelcome attentions."

"I think that's true," her friend said grimly. "But I don't envy him his job. Sally has long nails and digs in deep. She doesn't want to give up on him."

Jane sipped her coffee. "Such a situation can be very awkward in a town this small.

You keep on meeting the same people over and over."

"That's what makes it difficult," Maggie agreed. And then, with a bitter smile, she said bluntly, "I suppose you're like the others. You don't approve of my friendship with Boyd Davis."

Jane was caught by surprise. Putting down her cup, she said, "I don't think I said anything like that."

"You haven't mentioned him at all," Maggie said with irony. "I call that being overly tactful."

"I'm sorry."

"You needn't be," her friend said. "I suppose it is one way of handling it."

"I don't think you should take that attitude," Jane said. "I like Dr. Davis very much. And I'm sure when I get to know him better, my respect for him will increase. Dad claims he is a good doctor."

"And your father would know," Maggie agreed. "Boyd has become very important to me."

Jane stared at her. "How important?"

Maggie hesitated. "Terribly important."

She felt she might as well be blunt in her own questioning. So she asked, "Are you in love with him?"

"Yes. I think so."

"Will you marry him?"

Maggie stared out at the golfers, avoiding Jane's eyes. "He hasn't asked me yet."

"And if he does?"

"I'll make up my mind then."

"I see," Jane said. And then she added, "It seems to me you should give it some thought now."

Her friend continued to stare out of the window. "It would probably be wasted effort. Somehow, I don't think Boyd will ever ask me to be his wife."

"That could be kindness on his part, and wisdom."

Maggie turned to her almost fiercely. "I'm sick of good sense, calm judgment and wisdom! If marrying Boyd would be a foolish mistake, I'd like to make that kind of mistake!"

"I see," Jane said quietly. "Well, you've made it plain how you feel. What about Boyd?"

"He's holding back. In spite of Sally's gossip, we're merely good friends. We've made no plans, never discussed marriage. I guess it's hopeless."

"Perhaps if you went away from here —" Jane suggested.

"I'd go willingly," Maggie said with a strained look on her pretty face. "But I know Boyd doesn't want to leave. He's doing fine work here, building confidence in himself. He's not ready to move."

"There's no easy answer," Jane said. "I don't think there ever will be."

Maggie looked at her with hurt eyes. "He means more to me than any man I've ever known, and there has to be this barrier between us. How can anyone be so unlucky?"

Jane gave her a bitter smile. "I've asked myself that same question more than once."

"Forgive me," Maggie apologized. "I had no intention of spending the whole evening telling you how sorry I feel for myself."

"I'm glad to listen to your troubles," Jane said. "As I remember, it's part of a friend's duties."

The blonde girl's face brightened. "I think I feel better for having unburdened myself. So let's stop talking about me and give some time to your problems."

"I'm not involved in any romantic complications," Jane said with a faint smile.

"What about Steve Benson?"

"We're still friends."

Maggie's eyes opened wide. "Then you've seen him since you got back?"

"Once."

"What did he have to say?"

"The usual things. He hasn't changed any."

Maggie gave her a knowing look. "He's still in love with you. I'm sure of that. Every time we met during the years you were away, he did nothing but question me about you."

Jane smiled. "I think you're exaggerating."

"No, honestly. You two should never have broken up."

"I was the one who let him down," Jane reminded her.

Maggie shrugged. "Does that matter now? He's forgiven you."

"I'm not sure I deserve to be forgiven," Jane told her, "or even want to be. I need to do a lot of thinking before I consider marriage again."

"As long as you don't lose Steve a second time," Maggie warned her.

"So we both have our dilemmas," Jane said lightly. "How nice we have each other's shoulders to cry on."

Maggie drove her home around nine-thirty. They had talked a long while and filled one another in on happenings during their separation. Jane had enjoyed the evening, although she was filled with misgivings since learning that her friend was in love with the Negro doctor. There was so much chance this could lead to tragedy for both of them she had not felt able to encourage Maggie.

Mrs. Davis had been only too right in her fears.

Jane had a good night's rest, in spite of her unsettled state of mind, and the next morning left early to report for duty at the hospital. Her father was doing an appendectomy at nine, but there were no other operations scheduled for the morning.

"I suppose I should be thankful for that," he grumbled as he drove them to the hospital through the quiet streets of the early morning. "But I'm not. I'd like to be doing more surgery."

"Of course you would," she said. "But with such a skimpy staff, you're not geared to handle too many cases."

"We're withering on the vine," her father said. "As soon as the council works out some legal way to close us down, they'll do it. And then later they'll be sorry."

"Surely you would be invited to join the staff at the Bladeworth clinic," she suggested. "Then you could take your surgical patients down there. If they close the hospital, that would at least preserve your practice."

"I'm not thinking about my practice," her father said with a stubborn look on his aristocratic face. "I'm thinking of the hospital and all we've sacrificed in time and money to make it a success. Now this new crowd can talk of nothing but shutting the doors."

"Transportation has changed since the hospital was built," she reminded him. "The roads are much better, and there are many more cars, so that every little town doesn't need its own hospital."

"Offer that argument when you hear an ambulance siren coming all the way up the road from Bladeworth and then heading back again. A lot of time can be consumed on that return trip, even at top speed, and that time could mean the loss of a life."

Jane was ready to point out that an intern from the clinic usually rode in the ambulance and there were much better facilities in the modern new hospital at Bladeworth when a patient did arrive there. But at that moment they pulled into the hospital parking lot, so she said nothing.

Head Nurse McCumber greeted her like a long lost daughter. Miss McCumber was a solidly built woman with a beet-red face, horn-rimmed glasses and chronic foot trouble which made her walk with a sailor's rolling gait.

"It's good to have you back on the staff," she told Jane. "We've nearly two dozen patients and only three nurses on the day staff. I'll keep you on this floor with me."

Jane nodded. "That will give me time to get used to things again."

"Nothing much has changed," the head nurse assured her. "Except the new operating room, of course."

"I've seen it," Jane said.

"And the new doctors."

"I've met both Dr. Milton and Dr. Davis."

The older woman sat down at her desk with a sigh. "I guess they're both good enough men, but I have full confidence only in your father. We miss Dr. Silverwood."

Jane was careful to suppress the smile that came almost automatically in response to this. When she was a student, poor old Dr. Silverwood had been in his doddering eighties, and her father had expressed acid opinions of the veteran's capability on more than one occasion. But because Nurse McCumber remembered the old doctor from her own youth when he had been in his prime, she continued to regard him as the dean of practitioners.

"I remember Dr. Silverwood," was Jane's cautious comment.

The stout woman nodded dolefully. "We don't get men like him these days. I'm not saying Dr. Milton isn't talented. He is. And poor Dr. Davis has lots of ability, even if he is colored, which I'm sure he can't help. But it does make some of the patients uneasy with him."

"But don't they get over that feeling when they know him better?"

Miss McCumber gave her a surprised look. "Do you know that's exactly what does happen! How did you guess?"

"I've seen the same thing in the Boston hospitals," Jane said.

"Well, you would," the old nurse agreed. "They get doctors there from everywhere. Can't say I'd like it myself."

"How shall I begin?" Jane asked.

"You can start by checking on Walter Milligan and giving him his morning medications," Miss McCumber said. "He's your father's surgery patient, the one with the liver operation."

Jane was interested. "Dad told me about him. How is he coming along?"

"Well enough to be his usual mean self," the head nurse said indignantly. "You'll find out."

And Jane did. The sour-faced, stoutish Walter Milligan complained about everything she did for him. And when she attempted to give him his medicine, he offered an argument that it wasn't what he took regularly.

Jane managed to remain patient. She said, "It has to be right. It's clearly marked on your chart, along with the dosage."

He glared at her from his pillow. "Suppose they've gotten the charts mixed up?" he challenged her.

"They can't do that," she told him calmly. "Your chart has your name on it. Now will you take your medicine?"

He took it and then glared at her again. "So you're Doc Weaver's girl?"

"That's right."

"He's responsible for me being in here."

Jane smiled at the problem patient as she replaced his empty medicine glass on the tray she was carrying. "You mean he's responsible for your being alive."

"Same thing," Walter Milligan snapped. "I ruined my liver. Want to know how?"

"If you like," she said, deciding it was best to humor him.

"By drinking too much liquor," the sour-faced man said proudly. "Now what do you say to that?"

"I'd say you should stop."

"Don't know that I will," he said. "Man might as well be dead as have no fun."

"Cirrhosis isn't exactly my idea of fun," Jane told him.

He glared at her for a moment. Then he declared, "You remind me of my missus. You've got a sharp tongue in your head."

Jane was tempted to tell him his wife probably needed a sharp tongue for self-protection, but instead she said, "If you're comfortable, I'll go now."

"I got gas pains," he said. "And I want to talk to someone. You know who I am?"

"I should. It's on your chart. Mr. Walter Milligan."

"Councilman Walter Milligan," he corrected her. "And you know what? I'm going to close this place up."

"That will be bad for you if you have more liver trouble," Jane said.

"I can go to the new hospital at Bladeworth," he announced.

"You won't get any special treatment there," she warned him. "You're not a councilman in Bladeworth."

This seemed to strike home. He squinted at her. "You think Whitebridge should have its own hospital?"

"I think the hospital has been one the

111

town can be proud of," she said. "I can't answer for the town council. They know more about the business and financial problems of keeping it running than I do."

"That's fair enough," the sour-faced man said with a mild note of surprise in his voice. "I guess maybe you're right. Even if we do have to shut down Benson Memorial, we shouldn't feel too happy about it. We're losing something pretty good."

"I think so," she said. And she left him to think about it.

Her next patient was a summer visitor who had been stricken by a heart attack at one of the large summer hotels. He was a portly man in his late fifties and seemed uneasy in his oxygen tent. She administered to him and tried to make him as comfortable as she could. But she didn't like his color or the labored way he was breathing.

When she went back to the desk, she told Miss McCumber about this. The head nurse frowned. "It doesn't sound good."

"He should have a private nurse," Jane said.

"There isn't one available," Miss McCumber said, rising. "I'll take a look at the patient. Dr. Davis should be along any minute now. We can see what he thinks."

As it happened, Dr. Boyd Davis arrived before Miss McCumber came back from the heart patient's room. Jane quickly explained the situation to him.

Dr. Davis listened with a worried expression. "I was afraid of this," he said, and strode quickly down the corridor to the patient's room.

Jane took over the desk in Miss McCumber's absence. While she was there, her father's appendectomy case was brought up in the elevator. She had the patient assigned to a room near the desk where he could be easily watched. This was one of the problems that had to be kept in mind because of their skimpy staff.

By the time she'd looked after this, her father appeared on the scene. "The operation was a simple one," he told her. "There should be no complications."

"Fine," she said.

"Where's Miss McCumber?" he wanted to know.

"With Dr. Davis," she said. "The heart patient is having trouble."

"Oh?" Her father arched a white brow.

Just then both Dr. Davis and Miss McCumber came down the corridor together. The Negro doctor looked even more concerned than before and came straight to her father.

"Mr. Martin is in a bad state," he told Dr. Weaver.

"What are the signs? Do you think he's had another attack?"

"A minor one, perhaps," Dr. Davis said. "I believe we should ask Bladeworth to send up an ambulance for him."

Both Miss McCumber and her father seemed astounded at this. Her father's aristocratic face grew cold. "Are you suggesting we aren't competent to deal with a heart case here?"

"No, sir," Dr. Davis said quietly. "I'm remembering we don't have a heart machine. And one may be needed in this case. It could mean the difference between life and death for the patient."

"I'm not sure that I agree," her father said in an icy voice such as Jane had rarely heard him use. "Aren't you forgetting the risk involved in moving the patient?"

"I've tried to consider everything," the young Negro doctor said. "Mr. Martin happens to be my patient. I'll feel personally responsible if he should die here without the aid of a heart machine."

"Patients die in hospitals not equipped with them every day," her father argued.

"It's irresponsible to indict our service because we don't have one."

"And it's irresponsible to deny this patient the benefit of one when we can transfer him to Bladeworth," Dr. Boyd Davis maintained, a determined expression on his face.

Jane watched her father's reaction with some fear. She knew what an inward struggle he must be undergoing. And she also knew that the younger doctor was right. But this had to be a terrible blow to her father's pride. And he would also consider it ammunition for the council to use against him in their battle to close Benson Memorial.

At last Dr. Graham Weaver spoke in a choked voice. "You'll take full responsibility for the transfer?"

"Yes, sir."

"And you consider it absolutely necessary?" her father asked.

"Under the circumstances, yes," Dr. Davis said.

"Very well," her father said. "I'll put a call through to Bladeworth at once and have them come for the patient." Having said this, he turned away abruptly and headed for the elevator.

They all watched until the elevator door

closed after him. Miss McCumber's round face showed an expression of utter disbelief. Dr. Boyd Davis looked anything but happy.

He turned to Jane and shrugged. "I had no choice," he said. And he left them to return to the side of his patient.

Miss McCumber gave a deep sigh. "Well, I never thought I'd live to see the day!"

"Dr. Davis is right," Jane said. "We don't have a heart machine."

"Dr. Weaver didn't seem to think that so important," the head nurse said. "The patient may die because he's being moved in such a critical state."

"I still agree the chance should be taken," Jane said.

The eyes behind Nurse McCumber's thick glasses showed bewilderment. "It's like admitting Benson Memorial is out of date," she said.

Jane made no reply. She was certain her father must be thinking the same thing at the moment. And the sad part was that it was true.

CHAPTER SEVEN

Jane found her return to hospital duty in Whitebridge interesting. After nearly two years spent working in large hospitals in Boston, the set-up and routine of Benson Memorial seemed fairly primitive. And yet the hospital was well run for an institution of its size.

Her father made no mention to her of the patient sent to Bladeworth by Dr. Boyd Davis. But she learned from the Negro doctor that the patient had survived the trip to the larger hospital and was doing well. She was impressed by the authority Boyd Davis showed in his work, and she could tell he had a definite gift for diagnosis.

In the days that followed, she also had a chance to work under Dr. Wallace Milton and learn something about him. The handsome surgeon was quite different from Boyd Davis in his approach to patients. He was a trifle more aloof, but he did take a keen interest in those under his care. And she'd heard that in the operating room he was a perfectionist.

Miss McCumber had worked on several operating teams with Wallace Milton and confided to Jane, "He's slower than your father. But he is a fine surgeon, and extremely cautious."

Jane smiled. "Sometimes too much caution in a surgeon can be a fault. There are cases where a sudden decision to take a risk must be made."

"Of course that's true," the stout head nurse agreed. "And that's why your father always does so well. He works quickly, and he isn't afraid to try some radical move if there seems no other way. But Dr. Milton is talented, and I wouldn't be afraid to have him operate on me."

This was the highest praise a nurse could give a surgeon. So Jane took it for granted that Wallace Milton had proven himself in the operating room to Nurse McCumber's complete satisfaction.

Dr. Milton also seemed to have won over the bad-tempered Councilman Walter Milligan who had been his patient. The elderly man was almost ready to leave the hospital, and was an ambulatory patient now. He enjoyed conversation and moved from room to room visiting the patients whom he knew and who were well enough to talk to him. He also hailed members of the staff whenever they had a free moment.

Jane had an idea he made it a practice to watch for her and then waylay her with a long story. A typical example of this took place the morning of the day the old man was scheduled to be discharged. He halted her in the corridor and began complaining.

"No one has helped me pack my things," he said.

Jane smiled. "I'll get an aide to come by and assist you."

His bulldog faced showed a sour expression. "Why can't you do it? You've taken a dislike to me?"

"Of course not." She laughed. "But we do have quite a lot of patients to look after and only a few nurses to do it."

"Then why doesn't your father hire more nurses? A man pays enough in here. We ought to have the best."

Jane studied him with a twinkle in her eyes. "You have the answer to that, Mr. Milligan. You're on the council and voted to cut our budget."

The old man in the black and white striped dressing gown and blue pajamas looked uncomfortable. "Somebody has to watch expenses. If we didn't, they'd go so sky high no one would be able to pay his taxes."

"I'm sure the aide will do a good job helping you pack," Jane promised. "And we're going to miss you. Are you feeling well?"

"Best I have in years," the councilman said. "Only that young Dr. Milton says I got to cut down on my booze."

"Surely that isn't asking much," she said.

"It's asking plenty from me," he grumbled. "But I'll do it. That's a fine doctor. You paw was lucky to get him on the hospital staff. And when I'm able to attend a council meeting, I'm going to say that I know from experience this place is well run."

Jane lifted her eyebrows in a show of amused surprise. "Now that is a remarkable compliment, coming from you!"

He glared at her. "I wouldn't say it if I didn't think it was true. No one can get around me! And you're a good nurse."

"Thank you!"

"Matter of fact, being in here has sort of changed my views," Walter Milligan went on with a frown on his bulldog face. "I'm going to argue in favor of keeping Benson Memorial open when it comes to the budget meeting in September."

"Well, I only hope they'll listen to you," Jane said.

"I won't promise that," the old man said. "But I'll do what I can."

She thanked him and later reported the talk to her father. She was anxious to offer him some encouraging news. He'd seemed in a depressed state since Boyd Davis had referred the heart case to Bladeworth. So now she told him what the councilman had said.

Dr. Graham Weaver smiled wanly. "One thing about Milligan: he'll keep his word. If he's decided to battle for the hospital, nothing will stop him."

"He seemed very sincere about it. I think he's grateful for what you were able to do for him."

"It was touch and go after Dr. Milton brought him in," her father said. "And it took all our resourcefulness on the operating table to make a successful detour of that bad liver. To add to our problems, we had the knowledge that the operation doesn't always work."

She smiled. "It has in this case."

"The average seems to be about fifty percent good results," her father said. "It will be interesting to see what influence Milligan has on the council."

"He must be one of the senior members, isn't he?"

Her father nodded. "Yes. But I wouldn't say he has the most weight. Still, it's good to have him on our side."

Jane found working made her less restless and sensitive regarding her return to Whitebridge. With only her evenings left for social contacts, she nevertheless managed to see Maggie again in the week after returning to the hospital. And Steve called her several times for a date. Each time she found some excuse to refuse him, but she knew that couldn't go on. So she made up her mind to accept his offer to take her out when he phoned again. It was another decisive step toward a normal life.

Meanwhile, her days at the hospital seemed to become continually busier. The rush of summer visitors brought Benson Memorial a lot of extra patients. Quite a few of them were victims of minor accidents, and there were the usual quota of visitors with some type of holiday illness brought on by a change of food and water. Also, there were a few patients with more serious problems.

Catherine Barton was one of the latter group. The Bartons had been coming to the big resort hotel in Whitebridge for years. And although their only daughter Catherine was a few years younger than Jane, the two girls had come to know each other and be companions during the holiday months. The Bartons were wealthy and old to be the parents of an attractive redhead in her twenties such as Catherine. And it was to be expected that they doted on her and rather selfishly kept her with them all the time.

William Burton was retired, so he and his wife Eleanor, along with Catherine, spent a good part of the year moving from one resort to another. In the summer they stayed in New Hampshire or went to Europe, and in the fall and winter stayed in Virginia, Florida and sometimes Southern California. Catherine was an enthusiastic horsewoman and rode every day while in Whitebridge.

It was while she was riding on the hotel grounds one morning that she took a bad fall. The recreation director of the hotel brought her to the hospital at once in his station wagon. She was in a state of shock and seemingly in great pain. Both Jane's father and Dr. Boyd Davis were away from the hospital, but luckily Dr. Wallace Milton was on hand.

The handsome young doctor made a

thorough examination of the injured girl. Jane was with him to lend any assistance she could. Noting the paleness of her friend's face, along with the pain and tenderness of her abdomen, Jane knew the girl had suffered serious internal injuries.

A few minutes later, in the corridor outside Catherine Barton's room, Wallace Milton confirmed her fears. With a grave expression on his good-looking face, he said, "She's going to need an operation."

Jane eyed him anxiously. "I was afraid of that."

"You saw how she reacted to the examination," the young doctor said. "She's fallen on something that gave her a bad blow on the side. I imagine you know what's wrong."

Jane ventured a guess. "It could be a ruptured spleen."

"That's what it is," Dr. Milton said grimly. "There is internal hemorrhaging, and unless she's operated on as quickly as possible it could be fatal."

Jane said, "Her parents are waiting downstairs. You'd better let them know."

He nodded. "Yes. I'll want to talk to them. And I'll get Daisy to try to reach your father and Dr. Davis. We should schedule the operation for early afternoon at the latest."

"I'll tell Miss McCumber," Jane said.

Wallace Milton frowned. "She has her hands full up here. How long since you've scrubbed for the operating room?"

"Not long," Jane said. "I was in the O.R. most of the time at Peter Bent Brigham."

"Good girl," the handsome surgeon said. "We'll use you along with a circulating nurse." And he left her to go downstairs and interview the stricken girl's parents.

Jane had mixed feelings about being part of the operating team. She would be interested in seeing Dr. Milton and her father operate together but she was upset that the patient would be her friend, Catherine. She would have preferred it to be a stranger.

She went back into the shaded room of the pain-wracked girl and stood beside her bed. Catherine's vivid red hair was sprawled over the white pillow and her eyes were closed. She moved a little and moaned softly.

Then opening her eyes and seeing Jane again she managed a wan ghost of a smile. "Hello, Jane," she murmured. "Fine way for us to meet."

"You're going to be all right," she assured her.

Catherine closed her eyes. "Stupid!" she said bitterly.

"It was an accident. Don't worry. Dr. Milton will fix you up soon."

Catherine again looked up at her. "I got the handsome one," she said with a touch of the humor so characteristic of her.

Jane smiled. "You certainly did. Dr. Milton is very good looking."

"Have seen him at the hotel," Catherine said in her pain-filled tone. "What about Mother and Dad?"

"They'll be up to see you in a moment or two," Jane assured her. "They're talking to the doctor now."

And indeed the two worried elderly people did appear a moment or two later along with Dr. Wallace Milton. Jane guessed they would only be allowed to stay a short time. She left the room and went back to the desk where Head Nurse McCumber was coping with some medication orders.

When the stout woman had finished, she turned to Jane and said, "You're to work in the O.R. this afternoon. Dr. Milton hopes to operate at two-thirty."

"Fine," Jane said.

Miss McCumber sighed. "It's too bad about that pretty little Barton girl. You and she are friends, aren't you?"

"Yes," Jane said. "I hadn't seen her since

126

I came home. I don't think they arrived at the hotel until this week."

"Well, the sooner they operate the better," the head nurse said.

"I realize that," Jane agreed.

"You'd better take time off now and have your lunch," Miss McCumber went on. "You'll want to get back to make the operating room ready. Miss Cassiday will be the circulating nurse."

"I'll go right away then," Jane said.

Benson Memorial was too small a hospital to have an elaborate cafeteria. But one of the basement rooms adjoining the kitchens had been furnished as a recreation room, and it was there the staff had their meals.

When Jane went down, the room was empty except for her. After she'd taken her place at one of the several tables, a girl from the kitchen came out and took her food order. Jane studied the morning paper which was delivered to the hospital every day while she waited for the salad she'd decided on.

She was so absorbed in the paper she didn't realize that someone else had come into the room. And when Dr. Boyd Davis said, "Hello, Jane," in his pleasant voice, she looked up in surprise. He was standing

127

by the table, smiling at her and looking neat and professional in a gray summer suit.

"Hello," she said. "I was lost in the news."

He indicated the empty chair across from her. "Mind if I join you?"

"I wish you would," she said. "I dislike eating alone."

Boyd Davis laughed. "I don't mind myself. But my mother is the same way. She never has dinner until I get home, no matter how late I may be. And often I'm pretty late."

"Are you to be part of the operating team?" Jane asked.

"Yes. I'll be the anesthetist today. It's not a dangerous operation, as you know, but Dr. Milton and your father want everything to go right."

She said, "I've seen some nasty complications when disease of the spleen has been involved, especially in older people. Some of them have been on the operating table for longer than two hours."

The young Negro doctor looked thoughtful. "You're quite right," he said. "You never know until you open the patient up. In an accident of this sort there could be other damage."

128

"I hope not," Jane said. "Catherine is a dear friend of mine."

Boyd Davis raised his eyebrows. "I hadn't thought of that. But of course you'd know her. Her people have been coming to the hotel for years."

"Yes," she agreed. "And I'm scrubbing for Dr. Milton and my father."

He frowned. "Does that bother you? I mean, her being your friend?"

She shrugged. "I guess not. It did make me feel a little wary for a moment."

Their conversation was interrupted by the return of the waitress. She brought Jane's salad and milk. Boyd Davis ordered a ham sandwich and a cup of coffee.

Then he said, "This is the first time we've had a chance to talk together."

"So it is."

He smiled. "There's not much opportunity when you're on duty upstairs. And I'd like to know you better. Maggie has spoken so much of you, and with such enthusiasm."

Jane took a forkful of salad. "Maggie is very close to me."

"I know that," the young Negro doctor said evenly. "And I suppose it is no secret that she is close to me as well."

She glanced at him. "Not really."

129

"Do you approve of us?"

The blunt question caught her by surprise. She shrugged. "I think any true friendship is valuable to those concerned."

Dr. Boyd Davis chuckled softly. "Now that's what I call a tactful answer."

"I hope it was a truthful one as well," she said.

He smiled. "I'd say it was. Yes, I'll give you credit for that. I take you to be a truthful and sincere person. So you won't deny that Maggie and I have a problem in that she is white and I'm black."

Jane looked at him with a wrinkled brow. "You make it sound so final. Is a difference in color so important today?"

The young Negro doctor nodded. "Today, tomorrow, yesterday or whenever, a difference in race and color is always a major barrier between people. It's reasonable it should be. Maggie and I have been lucky enough to bridge that difference, but we can't expect other people to see things our way."

"You're being realistic about it," she said.

"If you're born black you soon get to be a realist." Boyd Davis smiled. "Mind you, I'm not complaining. I've been lucky."

She smiled. "I think it takes more than luck to earn a medical degree."

Their conversation was again interrupted by the waitress. When she left again, Boyd Davis resumed. "I want to apologize for my mother. She shouldn't have bothered you."

Jane had been sipping her milk. She put the glass down in surprise. "You know about that?"

"I found out."

"You mustn't be angry with her," Jane protested. "Your mother meant well, and we had an interesting conversation."

"That I'm sure of," Boyd Davis said with a mocking smile. "My mother is used to fighting hard for what she believes in. As you know, she doesn't believe my friendship with Maggie should continue."

Jane shrugged. "Could she be right? I mean for both your sakes."

He hesitated. "I've given that a good deal of thought. And you know what?"

"What?"

"I haven't been able to come to any conclusion."

Jane sighed. "Since I like you both, it's hard for me to advise you."

Boyd Davis had a mischievous twinkle in his eyes. "Get to know me better, Jane. Maybe you'll learn to hate me, and your problem will be resolved."

She shook her head. "I doubt it."

He gave her another of his keen looks. "You know what a bad marriage can do to people. Maggie has told me about you, the rough time you had."

She smiled bitterly. "My ideas of romance have undergone some radical changes."

"So now you're a cynic?"

"I hope not."

"I hope not, too," he said, reaching for his coffee. "An unfortunate mistake shouldn't be allowed to warp your life."

"So I've been told," she said.

He smiled across the table at her. "My mother liked you. My mother is a rare judge of people!"

"I'm pleased," she said. "How does your mother feel about Maggie?"

"Thinks she's a fine girl," Boyd Davis said, "but not for her son. So you see everyone has problems."

"I've found that out," Jane agreed.

Boyd Davis became more serious. "Even your father. He has this hang-up about the hospital. He doesn't want to see it closed, and I don't blame him. Just the same, he may be wrong. But still I want to be on his side, because he's a good man and a fine surgeon."

"I think so," she said softly.

Continuing in the same sober tone, the young Negro doctor said, "And yet I had to hurt him the other day by sending that patient to Bladeworth. I had no choice, but I knew I was hurting him and his cause."

She smiled. "I'm sure he understood."

"He was a big enough man to go along with my decision," Boyd Davis said. "You can learn a lot from men like him. The trouble is there aren't enough of them around."

"So it seems," she agreed.

He finished his coffee and stood up. "I have a call to make before I return for the operation. I'm glad we've had this chat. We must talk more often."

"Please," she said, rising. "It's been fun." And she walked toward the corridor door with him.

"I wouldn't worry too much about your girl friend, Catherine," Boyd Davis told her. "She'll be in good hands."

They parted at the elevator, and Jane went on to the operating room. The time had passed quickly, and it was almost two o'clock before she and Nurse Cassiday had everything ready for the two-thirty surgery.

The renovated room which was her father's particular pride seemed small and scantily equipped compared with the larger Boston hospital operating rooms. Yet everything that was required was there.

Jane and the older nurse went into the scrub room to greet her father and the two younger doctors and assist them with their gloves, smocks and masks.

Her father was the first to get there. He nodded to her brusquely. "I heard you were to be with us," he said.

"Miss McCumber decided," Jane told him.

"I'm glad you are," he said. "You must have seen a good many splenectomies at the Peter Bent Brigham."

"Quite a few," she agreed.

Her father sighed as he held out his hands so she could slip his robe on. "I've had another look at the little Barton girl. She's in a bad way. It could be we'll find more damage than we expect."

CHAPTER EIGHT

The younger doctors arrived, and Jane and Nurse Cassiday helped them prepare for the operating room. Jane assisted Dr. Wallace Milton with his rubber gloves, powdering his hands first.

He said, "I'll be glad to get this under way. Your father feels we've delayed as long as we dare."

She nodded as she put on his cap and mask. Her father had already taken his place in the operating room. They followed him in, and Jane noted that Catherine was already on the operating table, draped and sedated.

Dr. Graham Weaver turned to Dr. Boyd Davis at the anesthesia machine. "All right, Doctor," he said in his curt operating room tone.

As Boyd Davis administered the anesthesia, Jane glanced at the clock above the operating room doors and saw that it was two thirty-five. The tension in the brilliantly lighted room mounted. Boyd Davis nodded to her father, and he tested Catherine for sensitivity. There was no reaction to pain.

"Scalpel!" the senior surgeon said, and Jane handed it to him.

With Dr. Milton assisting, her father started the operation. His skilled hands moved with precision as he allowed the scalpel to pierce the skin.

Wallace Milton and her father worked for more than an hour to remove the ruptured spleen and clean up the surrounding damage. Dr. Boyd Davis kept a watchful vigil at the anesthesia machine. Hardly a word was spoken. Jane and Nurse Cassiday were kept busy. It was difficult for her to know how soon the surgery would come to an end.

Then her father said, "Transfusion!"

Jane started the blood flowing. A matching type had been readied before the surgery began. At the same time Dr. Boyd was carefully watching Catherine's respiration and pressure. Jane saw that her father's surgical gown was showing traces of perspiration. He had completed the major part of the work. Now Wallace Milton was closing the incision and putting in the last stitches. The wall clock showed four-ten.

Catherine was wheeled out of the operating room, and Jane's father took off his mask. His aristocratic face showed signs of weariness, but he was smiling.

"No need to worry," he said. "She'll respond nicely."

Dr. Wallace Milton had already doffed his mask. "I'm glad we didn't postpone surgery any longer," he said.

Her father nodded agreement. "The internal bleeding was building to a critical point." And the two men headed for the scrub room, still discussing the case.

Dr. Boyd Davis had shut off the anesthesia machine and now he came over to Jane with a broad smile on his intelligent face. "Well, Jane," he said, "that's the way we do it at Benson Memorial. Do we get your vote of approval?"

She smiled in return. "You surely do."

"With a surgeon like your father as head of the team, we'd have to be pretty stupid to blunder," the young Negro doctor said. "This period of working under him has been wonderful training for me."

Jane arched an eyebrow. "You speak almost as if it were over."

He looked embarrassed. "Sorry. I didn't mean it to sound like that."

"But you are thinking along those lines: that the hospital will close."

"To be honest, I suppose I am," he admitted. "But then you never can predict such things."

Jane remained with Nurse Cassiday to clean up the operating room after the doctors left. It took quite a little time, and when she finished she changed and left the hospital for the day.

She hadn't brought her car to work and planned to take a leisurely walk home. But just as she reached the sidewalk outside the front entrance to the hospital, a sedan came down the driveway, and the driver touched his horn to capture her attention. She turned and saw it was Dr. Wallace Milton gesturing to her to join him.

With a smile she went over and looked at him behind the wheel. "I thought I'd walk home," she said. "It's such a lovely warm afternoon."

"Let me give you a ride," he insisted. "You'll be exhausted if you walk all the way."

"It's really not that far," she protested. But rather than seem unfriendly, she got into the front seat of the car beside him.

His handsome face showed pleasure. "I'd expect you to be tired after our strenuous afternoon," he said as he headed the car into traffic.

"I do feel a little weary," she admitted.

"You're a first class scrub nurse," the young doctor went on. "Your Boston training shows."

"It was an easy team to work with today," she said. "I was impressed by the way you all worked together."

"That young woman was in bad shape," he said, guiding the car along the crowded street.

"Catherine is a wonderful girl and an only child," she told him. "It would have been tragic to have anything happen to her."

"She seemed to have a lot of charm," the handsome doctor agreed. "It is rather hard to judge exactly. She was in a good deal of pain from the time I first saw her. But even under those conditions her personality came through."

"Will her convalescence take up much of her summer?"

"She'll be in the hospital only about ten days if all goes well," he said. "But it will probably be the end of the summer before she can resume full normal activity."

"Poor Catherine!" Jane said. "She'll miss most of the summer's fun."

The handsome doctor at the wheel smiled. "Don't let that upset you too much. She could have died on that table this afternoon."

"Of course you're right," Jane agreed at once.

"She'll be able to do some sunning and perhaps a little dancing or shuffleboard," he went on. "But riding, golfing and swimming will be out."

Jane smiled. "I'll let you be the one to tell her that."

"I'll muster my best bedside manner," he promised. "How are you adapting to Whitebridge?"

"I'm doing very well, thanks."

He glanced at her. "I haven't seen you at the country club since you've come home. Are you like my wife, not too interested in the town's social doings?"

"I've been there once with Maggie Grant," she said.

Wallace Milton nodded, his eyes on the street ahead. "Ah, yes. Boyd's girl friend."

Jane frowned slightly, not certain she liked his inflection. She said, "She and Boyd Davis are friends, but I don't think they deserve the smears that some people have spread about them. Your own friend, Sally Benson, seems to have a particular grudge against Maggie."

She saw the crimson mount in the young

doctor's face. Without glancing her way, he said tautly, "I hope you don't think I was agreeing with Sally's attitude in the matter. Actually, I've given her a couple of reprimands because of what she's said about Boyd and Maggie."

"I'm sure she deserved them," Jane said stoutly, "especially since she's anything but discreet herself."

This time the young doctor gave her a brief searching glance. "I want you to know I've given Sally no encouragement," he said.

"I'm sure she doesn't need any," Jane said.

Dr. Wallace Milton wheeled his car into the street where her father's house was located. "Sally is a very mixed-up girl," he said.

"I know that," she agreed.

"She doesn't seem to be able to make up her mind what she wants from life."

"That's probably because she's always had far too much," Jane said. "I'd call her thoroughly spoiled."

"You like Steve better?" he suggested.

She shrugged. "Steve and I have known each other since we were children. I don't think his wealth and position in town have spoiled him."

"I agree," the young doctor said, bringing his car to a halt in front of the slate-gray house. "He is even careful about using his powers as mayor. I think he's been very fair in the debate about the hospital."

"I imagine he would be," she said.

"I've tried to help Sally a little," the young doctor went on with a troubled look on his handsome face. "It's very difficult. She is too quick to construe interest as something deeper."

Jane smiled ruefully. "I understand."

He gave her a knowing look. "It's pretty much an old story in town that I have serious home problems. But I'm not the sort to carry on an affair or break up a marriage lightly. Sally doesn't seem to realize this, or else she prefers to ignore it."

"She can be very determined."

"So I've discovered," he said sadly. "My only protection is to give up seeing her entirely."

"You're wise," she said.

He sighed. "I've probably talked too much. I'd appreciate your forgetting most of what I've said. It's a relief to be frank with someone."

"I'll promise to have a bad memory," she

said with a smile. "And thanks for the drive."

"I enjoyed talking to you," the young doctor said. "As soon as Ruth is feeling better, I promise to arrange that dinner party."

"It sounds nice," Jane said politely, getting out of the car.

Wallace Milton waved as he drove on. Jane watched him go with a feeling of sympathy.

When she entered the living room, her Aunt Emily came to the doorway leading to the kitchen and gave her a wise look. "I see you have a new boy friend," she said.

Jane blushed. "Nothing like that. Dr. Milton drove me home from the hospital."

Aunt Emily's plain face showed interest. "For a minute I thought you might be trying to beat Sally Benson's time. That girl has set her cap for young Milton."

"But he has a wife!"

"Don't think that bothers Sally," Aunt Emily said with derision. "It just adds to the challenge. Where's your father?"

"I expect he's still busy at the hospital. Catherine's operation took nearly all afternoon. He was bound to get behind with his patients."

"You never can be sure when he'll get

143

home these days," Aunt Emily complained. "He comes at all hours."

"The operation would normally have been scheduled for the morning, but Dad didn't think Catherine should be kept waiting that long. As it turned out, it's lucky they didn't postpone the surgery. She had bad internal bleeding."

"How did she come through the operation?"

"She'll be all right. But her summer will be ruined."

Aunt Emily's expression was grim. "Another case of someone with too much money and not enough to do. If she hadn't been riding that horse, she'd never have had that accident."

"Riding is a fine sport," Jane argued. "You shouldn't talk like that. Catherine didn't deliberately ask for the accident. It just happened. You shouldn't blame her. She's a lovely girl."

"I know all about that," her aunt said. "And I still say she's too filthy rich. Most of the summer people are."

Jane laughed. "Don't complain about them. They provide a good share of Father's practice."

"I'll admit that," her aunt said. "But I don't have to be happy about it." And then, abruptly changing the subject, "Another of your male conquests just phoned you. He said he'd be calling back."

Jane looked surprised. "Who?"

"Who do you suppose? It was Steve Benson. He said he'd phone back in fifteen or twenty minutes."

Before Jane had a chance to start upstairs, the phone rang, and it was Steve. The first thing he asked was, "How is Catherine Barton?"

"She's going to recover nicely," Jane assured him.

"I'm glad to hear that," the young mayor said. "Catherine is one of my favorite persons. And now we'll get down to the subject of you."

Jane laughed. "I'm in perfect health."

"I wasn't referring to your health," Steve said. "I'm calling again to ask you for a date. I suppose you're going to refuse."

"How can you be so sure?"

"You have every other time I've phoned," he reminded her. "What about coming with me to the dinner dance at the country club on Saturday night?"

She hesitated for only a moment. "I think I'd like it."

"What about that?" he asked in awe. "And I was so certain you'd say no."

"I will if you want me to."

"Of course I don't want you to," he said hastily. "It just comes as a surprise. I'll pick you up around seven so we'll have time for cocktails first. It will seem like old times."

"Indeed it will," she agreed happily.

Within a couple of days Catherine Barton was over the worst of the pain and discomfort of her serious operation. And on the third day, when Jane entered her room, she found the attractive redhead sitting up and smiling.

"Welcome, Nurse Weaver," was Catherine's greeting. "I'm not used to seeing you in uniform."

"And I'm not used to seeing you in a hospital room." Jane laughed. "But I must say you're not looking much like a patient today."

Catherine was still pale but radiant. "I didn't think I felt like getting up, but Dr. Milton insisted that I should."

"It's the procedure," Jane assured her friend. "You'll get better more quickly."

"That's happy news," Catherine said with twinkling eyes, "though I can't say how I'm going to hide the scar from this six-inch incision in a bikini."

"Use body make-up," was Jane's advice.

"You'd be surprised how many gals do."

"Thanks for the good cheer," the redhead said. "My parents think your father and the other doctors are the greatest. And they're planning to spend an extra month at the hotel so I'll have a chance to get some sports in before I leave."

"September is one of our best months," Jane said. "You won't be sorry you decided to stay."

Catherine gave her a wondering look. "And they tell me you're back here to live."

"At least I'm back." Jane smiled. "Whether I stay or not depends."

"On Steve?" Catherine asked.

"On a lot of things," Jane said, "though Steve is taking me to the dance on Saturday."

"Lucky you!" was Catherine's comment. "I've always been strong for Steve myself, but he doesn't know I'm alive."

"I wouldn't say that," Jane told her. "The first thing he did when he phoned me the other night was ask about you."

"I'm encouraged," the girl in the easy chair said. She made a small motion and then winced. "Every so often I get a reminder why I'm here."

"It will hurt for a time."

"What a handsome doctor I have,"

Catherine said. "If I didn't know he was married, I'd be after him right this minute."

Jane gave her an amused look. "Pretty big ambitions for an invalid."

"I mean it," the other girl said. "Wallace Milton has charm! And that graying hair at his temples really sends me."

"Don't let it send you too far," Jane advised. "He isn't the type for casual romances. And Sally Benson has already given him enough headaches."

"So I've heard," the scintillating redhead said eagerly. "You must tell me more about it."

"Gossip is not on your medication list," Jane said dryly. "If you don't mind, we'll postpone it until later."

"You're the nurse," Catherine said amusedly. "And I still say Wallace Milton is a handsome man."

Jane was not surprised that Catherine had been impressed by the young doctor's charm; most of his female patients felt exactly the same way about him. She had dinner at the club with Maggie that night and told the blonde girl about it.

Maggie looked wise. "Poor Wallace Milton! He's in enough trouble already. I hear Sally phones him all the time and threatens him with all sorts of nonsense

148

because he refuses to see her."

"How did you find that out?" Jane asked in surprise.

"I have ways." The blonde girl smiled. "The Milton housekeeper happens to be a friend of the woman who comes in to do the work at our place two days a week. She says that whenever the housekeeper gets Sally on the line, she listens on the extension when the doctor takes the call."

"I call that pretty sneaky!" was Jane's indignant reaction.

"Sneaky or not, it makes for some fascinating listening, according to the housekeeper," Maggie said. "Sally is now threatening to commit suicide if Dr. Milton throws her over."

"But he never has been serious about her!"

"Everyone in town seems to realize that except Sally."

"What about his wife?" Jane asked.

Maggie looked at her oddly. "You mean to say you haven't met Ruth yet?"

"No. Dr. Milton has mentioned her several times. But she doesn't seem to show herself in town much."

"That she doesn't," Maggie agreed with a grim expression. "All I can tell you is that Ruth Milton is in such a bad mental state she'd suspect any female in town of flirting with her husband as quickly as she'd blame Sally. She's muddled and crazily jealous of him. They say she's been that way ever since her breakdown."

"I suppose that's why he came here."

"What other reason could there be?" Maggie said.

"It's dreadful for him," Jane worried.

"Don't you go getting a crush on him as well," Maggie warned her. "You've made your mistake."

Jane blushed. "I didn't mean it that way."

Maggie smiled. "I know you didn't, and I shouldn't be so catty. The truth is: I'm pretty much on edge these days."

"It doesn't matter."

Maggie looked at her across the table. "Boyd says you were marvelous in the operating room the other day."

"He wasn't half-bad himself," Jane said.

"Boyd isn't lavish with his praise, especially when it comes to people in his field, but he went all out about you."

"We get along well," Jane said. "Steve is bringing me here to the club for the Saturday dance. I was going to suggest you and Boyd join us."

Maggie's expression changed. "That

wouldn't work," she said quietly. "I've already spoken privately to Henry about it. He says he has strict rules to bar coloreds from the dining room."

Jane was shocked. "I don't think of Boyd Davis as colored. I think of him as a person I like and a fine doctor."

"Henry feels the same way," Maggie said. "But as headwaiter, he has been given instructions by the club committee and has to carry them out. Boyd is a Negro, and so he isn't welcome here."

"It's stupid," Jane fumed, "especially since he's doctor to a lot of the members who made the rule."

"I agree," Maggie said with a shrug. "I was going to turn in my membership card. But then I realized what a foolish, futile gesture that would be. Everyone would know I did it because I feel as I do about Boyd. They'd pity me, but they wouldn't change their minds about the rule."

"They're much too smug for that!"

Maggie's eyes met hers. "So would I have been a few years ago," she said. "And I think you would have been as well. Let's be honest with ourselves. It's only because we know Boyd that we've changed."

Jane was caught by surprise. With a

stunned feeling, she asked her friend, "Are we such snobs?"

"It's not snobbery," Maggie said. "It's a matter of social custom and acceptance. Changes of this kind come slowly, even though I'm sure they're bound to come. For the present, I think it best to defer to the club rules."

"Does Boyd know about this?"

"Yes. And he agrees. It's an old story to him. He finds it somewhat amusing," Maggie said with a touch of bitterness.

"I'm not sure I would if I were in his place."

Maggie offered her a weary, wise glance. "But then how lucky we are that we are not in his place," she said.

CHAPTER NINE

On Saturday evening Jane took particular care dressing. It was her first date with Mayor Steve Benson since her return to Whitebridge. And she knew the dinner dances at the country club on Saturdays were well attended.

She'd had her hair done in the late afternoon, and now she selected a stylish blue dress with a net top which she'd bought from a famous shop in Boston. It was her best dress, and she felt this was the night to let Whitebridge see it.

When she came downstairs to wait for Steve, she found her father seated in an easy chair in the living room with a book. He glanced up at her and his aristocratic face took on an appreciative smile.

"I like your hair-do and dress," he said. "You'll really be noticed tonight."

She smiled, holding the fur-collared sweater she had brought along, and stood before him to be admired. "After wearing a plain white uniform all week, it's fun to dress up," she said.

"Steve and you will make a handsome couple," her father observed. "But then you always did."

Jane went over and kissed him on the forehead. "Tell Aunt Emily not to wait up for me. I may be late."

"Won't make any difference what I tell her; she'll stay up as long as she likes," Jane's father warned her. And jerking his head toward the upper part of the house from which the sounds of television were coming loudly, he added, "And don't forget this is the night she watches the late show. So she'll be up till all hours anyway."

"You get to sleep at least," Jane admonished him. "You've had a hard week. And you look worn out."

He chuckled. "You don't know what a hard week is. You should have seen what we used to do when the hospital first opened. I operated every morning and made a whole string of house calls as well."

"You were younger then."

The eyes under the shaggy white brows took on an expression of sadness. "You're right! The hospital was new then, too. Now we're both headed for the scrap heap."

Jane gave him a reproving look as she draped the sweater over her shoulders. "I'll not offer an opinion about the hospital," she said. "But I'll assure you I don't see you as scrap heap material after the way you performed in surgery the other afternoon."

"That was nothing," Dr. Graham Weaver said with a lofty gesture of dismissal. "In the old days I'd do three operations like that in a morning."

Steve came to the door, and Jane hurried over to let him in. He was wearing a Palm Beach jacket and matching trousers and looked very much the enterprising young mayor and businessman. He gave her an admiring glance and said, "That's a knockout of an outfit, Jane."

"I'm glad you like it," she said demurely. "Do you want to say hello to Dad?"

"I never miss a chance to do that," Steve said, coming in. He entered the living room and crossed to her father. "Good evening, sir. I suppose you've noticed how lovely your daughter looks tonight."

Her father got to his feet, shaking hands with Steve and smiling. "I guess she made a special effort because this is her first big evening out since she's returned to Whitebridge," he said.

Jane looked amused. "Please," she begged. "This dress isn't all that grand."

"But you are," Steve insisted, going over to admire her again.

"We'd better get started or we'll be late," Jane suggested, embarrassed by the attention she'd drawn and anxious to get away.

Her father followed them out to the steps. "Have a good time," he told them. "And if there's a polka, dance it for me."

As Steve drove her off in the convertible, he said, "Your dad is one of my favorite people."

She glanced at him behind the wheel. "I hope you remember that when the hospital budget comes up."

He looked worried. "I'll do what I can. I promise. But more and more it's out of my hands. You've won one new booster for the hospital, but the rest are still opposed to it being kept operating. How did you get around Councilman Walter Milligan?"

She laughed. "Good treatment, I'd say. He promised he'd be on our side when he was discharged."

"And he meant it. He'll do some good. He's a hard old nut to oppose. But right now it's only Milligan and myself against the rest. And I can only vote if there's a tie."

Jane frowned as they swung out on the road leading to the country club. "Then that means the hospital will almost surely be closing?"

"I'm afraid so," Steve said. "Of course the closing won't be effective until the beginning of next year."

"It's really only a short time until January first, even if it is only July," she worried. "There's not enough warning to give my father a chance to adapt properly to the situation."

Steve turned the car into the asphalt parking lot of the country club. "I doubt if he'll be able to adjust anyway," he said. "It's going to be a bad experience for him no matter when it comes."

"I suppose you're right," she said unhappily. "But we are doing good work at Benson Memorial. It seems to me your council should rethink their plans."

The rows of cars in the parking lot indicated a big crowd was attending the Saturday dinner dance. When Jane entered the club lobby on Steve's arms, she was conscious of a number of eyes fastened on them.

They joined a group having cocktails by the circular bar on the porch. One of the first couples Jane noticed were Dr. Wallace Milton and his wife. The young doctor was looking as handsome as ever in a white jacket with black bow tie. But it was the rather worn-looking woman at his side who drew Jane's attention.

It had to be Ruth Milton making one of her rare appearances socially. She was wearing a severe black dress that did little to flatter her gaunt appearance. Jane could tell that once Ruth Milton might have been considered a near-beauty. She had good bone structure. But this was spoiled by her extreme thinness and the coldness of her large brown eyes. Her brownish hair was drawn back straight and caught in the back; this also was unflattering and emphasized the gaunt hollows of her cheeks and temples.

At the moment she was holding a tall glass of amber liquid in her right hand, her eyes nervously taking in those standing near her. There was no hint of a smile on her drawn face, no apparent communication between her and the husband she was standing beside.

Seeing Jane, Wallace Milton touched his wife's arm and said something to her in a low voice. Then he led her forward to join Jane and Steve. Ruth Milton came with obvious reluctance.

Her husband, on the other hand, was all smiles. "Ruth, I want you to meet Jane Weaver," he said.

Ruth Milton responded by studying Jane with a somewhat derisive smile. "Of course, Dr. Weaver's daughter. The one you raved about, who did so fabulously in the operating room the other day."

"She's the one," Wallace Milton agreed happily. "And of course you know Steve, our mayor."

Ruth Milton eyed Steve coolly. "Of course," she said. "But I think of him mostly as Sally's brother."

There was a second of awkward silence before Steve said quickly, "I believe that's how many people remember me. The penalty I pay for having an attractive sister." And he smiled.

Ruth Milton did not smile. Jane noticed the unhappy woman's hand trembling slightly as she raised the glass to her lips to take a sip from it.

Then Ruth said, "My husband is in full agreement with you. He considers Sally most attractive." And she turned a cold glance Jane's way and added, "But Wallace is rather impartial. He has an eye for any pretty girl."

Jane felt there was no answer to that. A glance at the doctor's shadowed face told her that he was feeling the strain.

He forced a smile for her and Steve,

saying, "If you'll excuse us, we have some other friends to speak to." He touched Ruth's elbow and guided her away. They had gone only a few steps when she dropped her glass. It fell to the floor, splashing its liquid contents widely and splintering.

The unfortunate accident brought annoyed cries from nearby females threatened by the spilled liquor and the broken pieces of glass. A steward came forward at once with a cloth and bucket to get rid of the hazardous mess. Wallace Milton quickly led his wife off to a deserted portion of the porch, away from the group having cocktails.

Steve gave Jane a troubled glance. "That was a nice exhibition," he said.

"I don't think he should have brought her here," she replied. "That woman is ill."

"You don't have to sell me on that idea," the young mayor said grimly. "Have you ever seen her drive her car?"

"No. This is my first meeting with her."

"I'd forgotten," he said. "Well, she drives like a lunatic. I've spoken to Milton about it. She almost ran a little girl down a month or so ago. The child was playing in the street, but there was no excuse for Ruth Milton driving at the speed she was.

If the child had been killed, she'd have been in a bad spot."

"I don't think the doctor has much control over her," Jane said. "The only way he could change her driving habits would be to take her car from her. And that would mean a series of quarrels."

Steve still watched the two at the other end of the porch. "He caters to her far too much. He's undoubtedly pleading with her to behave now when he should be taking her home."

"It's easy for us to criticize," she pointed out gently. "But he's in a difficult position."

Steve frowned. "I know that. Well, let's not allow it to spoil our evening."

And they didn't. When at last they were seated at a table for two in the main dining room, Steve told her, "I see Milton and his wife just a few tables behind you. She doesn't look any happier than she did earlier."

"I hardly imagine there will be any change in her," Jane said. "She has some mental trouble. Dr. Milton should see that she gets treatment."

"My guess is he's about given up," was Steve's opinion. "Not that she's entirely to blame. My darling sister, Sally, hasn't helped matters by running after the doctor the way she has."

"Is she here tonight?" Jane asked, glancing around.

"Not yet. She's coming later for the dance. Some fellow from Rangely, a summer visitor, is bringing her." He gave Jane a meaningful look. "I hope she behaves."

They enjoyed dinner, and then the music and dancing began in the adjoining room. Jane and Steve went in for the first medley. It lasted nearly fifteen minutes, and the floor became filled with couples. The overhead lights had been turned out, and only two or three subdued spotlights were focused on the ballroom floor. It was hard to pick out couples in the shadowy atmosphere of the big room.

Jane pressed close to Steve and enjoyed the music. He was a good dancer, and it had been so long since they had danced together she'd forgotten what an excellent team they made.

He spoke in her ear, "This makes me forget all the nights we missed being together."

"I want to forget them," she murmured, "and just remember here and now."

When the music finally ended, Steve

took her out on the patio that faced the golf course. In the distance, high over the mountain peaks, a full orange moon had risen against a cloudy sky. Without a word he took her in his arms for a lingering kiss.

After it ended, he said, "Have you thought over what we talked about when we were last together?"

She smiled up at him. "We talked about a lot of things."

"Only one important thing. I asked you to marry me."

She shook her head. "I told you I wouldn't be rushed," she warned him.

"So you did," he said with bitter humor. "But I don't think I am rushing you. I feel we've lost two years already. Why lose any more time?"

Her eyes looked up into his. "I promise you if I marry anyone, it will undoubtedly be you. But I'm just not ready."

Steve looked unhappy. "Why?"

"So many reasons," she said helplessly, "I can't itemize them. My own mixed-up feelings, the past I haven't forgotten, my father's problems —" She stopped and with a sigh said, "Need I go on?"

Steve stared down at her. "I haven't heard a good reason yet."

Jane gave a forlorn smile and linked her

arm in his. "You wouldn't admit it if you had," she told him. "Let's go back inside."

When they danced again, the floor was not so crowded. Suddenly Jane saw a familiar couple only a short distance from them. It was Wallace Milton with Sally Benson in his arms. The young doctor looked unhappy, but Sally was smiling contentedly as she pressed close to him while they circled the floor to the music.

Jane whispered urgently to Steve, "Look, behind us!"

He swung around so he could see the dancing couple. At once his face showed alarm.

"What can we do?" Jane asked.

"When the music ends, we'll stop close to them," Steve said, "and I'll ask to change partners. It will give me a chance to try to talk some sense into the silly head of that sister of mine."

"Will she dance with you?"

"She'd better," Steve said savagely. "If they keep on this way, we'll have Ruth Milton out on the floor indulging in a hair-pulling contest with her."

"It could happen," Jane admitted with despair.

They timed it so that when the music stopped for a moment, they wound up next to Sally and Wallace Milton. Sally saw them, and an angry expression crossed her attractive face.

Steve took no notice of this. Taking his sister's arm, he told Wallace Milton, "We'll swap partners for this one."

Sally glared at him. "What makes you think so?"

The music had resumed, and Steve already had her in his arms in a dance position. "I've been looking forward to it," he said as he led her off.

Jane found herself in the young doctor's arms. As they danced, he said, "Steve saw my plight."

"How did she get you on the floor?" Jane asked.

Wallace Milton looked weary. "Ruth refused to dance. Then Sally came along with this stranger who brought her. I thought everything would be all right, since she had an escort. Instead of dancing with him as I expected she would, she left him stranded with Ruth and insisted on going on the floor with me."

"Wasn't that a bit obvious?"

"Sally hasn't been bothering with subtleties lately," he worried. "She even calls my place."

Jane frowned up at him. "Doesn't she realize what she's doing is doubly wrong because of your wife's breakdown?"

"I've tried to tell her that," he said. "She's impossible! She just refuses to listen."

"The best thing you can do now is to take Ruth home as quickly as possible," she said. "I don't think she can be enjoying herself."

"She isn't," the young doctor agreed. "When we dance by where she's sitting, we can leave the floor. It will give me a chance to get started home before the dance ends."

Jane nodded, and when they came to the table where a pale-faced Ruth sat in grim silence with the uncomfortable young man who had rashly escorted Sally to the dance, they broke away from the circling groups.

Wallace Milton went over to his wife and, with a smile, said, "It's late, and most of the fun is over. I think we should leave."

Ruth wasn't looking at him but was staring at Jane with sheer hatred in her too bright brown eyes. She said, "Are you sure you can tear yourself away from Miss Weaver?"

"I suggest we go," the young doctor said firmly, ignoring her remark.

Ruth Milton got to her feet and gave Jane one final malicious glance before turning to leave. The young doctor glanced at Jane with a silently mouthed good night, then quickly followed his wife.

The surprised young man who was Sally's escort tried to make the best of a bad situation by asking Jane, "Would you like to finish the dance with me?"

"Why not?" she asked, managing a smile despite her tension.

He apparently was tongue-tied with embarrassment to such a point he was unable to think of another word to say. However, he happened to be a fair dancer, so she got through the next difficult few minutes.

Steve joined them when the music ended. An angry-faced Sally at his side at once began asking where the young doctor had gone. When her escort indicated he had left to go home, Sally abruptly hurried off to try to reach him before he escaped from the clubhouse.

Steve gave Jane a despairing glance and said, "We've done our good deed for the night. Let's get in the last few dances on our own." And they left the utterly bewildered young man from Rangely standing alone.

Jane smiled at Steve. "I don't think that fellow will forget tonight."

"I'm not sure I will," Steve said as they resumed dancing.

On Monday Jane took time to tell some of what had happened to a rapidly recovering Catherine Barton. The red-haired girl enjoyed it all and begged her for the details, even wanting to know what various people had been wearing.

"I'm so frustrated being cooped up here," Catherine said, looking outrageously pretty in a Chinese red kimono with an exotic pattern through it.

Jane smiled. "You'll be out of the hospital in a few days."

"But I won't be able to do a thing but sit on the hotel verandah and watch other people having fun," Catherine mourned.

"The month will go by fast," Jane said. "You'll be surprised."

The redhead sighed. "Well, at least I'll have the handsome Dr. Milton to call on me for checkups," she said.

"Go easy with that," Jane warned. "He has a very jealous wife."

It was another busy week at the hospital. And to complicate matters Miss McCumber, the stout head nurse, twisted her ankle, and this kept her away from work for three days. Jane had to assume her duties and carry on her own work as well.

Dr. Boyd Davis brought in a badly

burned youth who had been working in one of the hotel kitchens when a boiler of fat had splashed over him. He was in a pathetic state, with second and third degree burns over a large area of his right side. Jane despaired of the boy's life, but the Negro doctor battled gallantly to save him.

Jane returned to the hospital several nights to do private duty with the unfortunate youth. Boyd Davis came in regularly as soon as his office hours were over. And finally his unswerving dedication to the case paid dividends. The boy began to show slow signs of recovery.

"Chalk up another small victory for Benson Memorial," Boyd told Jane with a smile as they stood in the corridor outside the youth's room.

"I'd give the credit to you personally," she said.

"What about the private duty time you put in on the case?" the doctor wanted to know. "I tell you I can't see you collecting any pay for that."

Jane's eyes twinkled. "Worry about that when I present my bill, Dr. Davis."

The tall dark man's eyes shone with pleasure. "I tell you my mother is never wrong about a girl. That's the truth! She told me about you right off!"

Jane enjoyed the easy camaraderie she had with Boyd Davis. And she could understand why Maggie felt as she did about the talented Negro doctor. But like Boyd's mother, she couldn't see the happiness they deserved ahead for them if they married. It was one of the several problems that continued to worry her.

The word about the developments concerning the hospital also continued to be ominous. And as rumors kept cropping up that Benson Memorial would get its death blow at the September council meeting, she saw a deterioration in her father's health. He had seemed to age even since her return home. And Aunt Emily continually lamented his poor appetite.

Then there was the question of whether she would marry Steve or not. She'd seen the young mayor several times since the country club dance, and on each occasion he'd brought the matter up.

And on top of all this, she had discovered she'd made a new enemy. Twice when she'd been walking in town, Ruth Milton had passed her in her car. The young doctor's wife had deliberately snubbed her each time.

The matter was brought to a crisis one evening early in August. Jane was at home reading when the phone rang. Her father had gone back to his office at the hospital, and her aunt was upstairs watching television, so she answered the phone herself. It was Dr. Wallace Milton at the other end of the line, and he seemed badly upset.

"I need your help," he told her. "Don't refuse me. I'll call for you in ten minutes." And he hung up without giving her a chance to say a word.

CHAPTER TEN

The urgency in Dr. Wallace Milton's tone left Jane no choice but to take this call seriously. She went upstairs and interrupted her aunt at the television set to let her know she was going out.

"What time will you be back?" Aunt Emily wanted to know as she turned down the volume on the Western action story she'd been watching.

Jane shrugged. "I can't say. I shouldn't be long."

Aunt Emily regarded her with some suspicion. "You made up your mind very suddenly, didn't you?"

"Someone phoned," Jane said truthfully. "Tell Dad I'll be home early."

"And then if you aren't, he'll start fussing," her aunt complained.

"I will be," Jane promised.

She snatched a sweater from the closet in her room and hurried downstairs. Then she went out to the street and waited for the young doctor to arrive. It was already dark and getting chilly, so she put on her sweater and watched impatiently for car lights to turn into the block.

Finally he came, and she quickly got in beside him. Even in the darkness of the car's interior, she sensed the tension in him. Staring at him with worried eyes, she asked, "What's wrong?"

"Sally," he said, his handsome profile shadowed with concern as he headed the car back to the main street once more. "She's really pulled a prize boner this time!"

"What now?"

"She's been threatening all sorts of crazy things," Wallace Milton said grimly. "She called me early tonight and threatened she would commit suicide if I wouldn't agree to leave Ruth for her."

"No!"

"Of course I didn't take her seriously," he went on as he guided the car out of town in the direction of the river. The dash light reflected on his tense features. "But she called a second time and told me she had taken an overdose of sleeping tablets. I knew she wasn't bluffing, because the tablets were beginning to take effect, and it showed in her voice."

"Did you get to her in time?"

He nodded. "Barely. The little fool didn't seem to realize how close she had come to carrying out her threat. Now she's in a state of panic, and I don't dare leave her alone."

"Where is she?"

"At a summer cottage by the river. It's one her family owns and rents to tourists. It's been empty the past couple of weeks. Once I met her there and tried to talk some sense into her."

Jane gave a deep sigh. "Sally will do anything to get her own way."

"She's not getting it this time," the young doctor warned, his eyes on the road ahead. "I've told her that I will not desert Ruth under any circumstances. We had a good marriage once. We're having trouble now because of her illness, but it can't be blamed on her. Sally refuses to see that."

"What do you want me to do?" Jane asked him.

He gave her an appealing glance. "It would help me a great deal if you'd stay the rest of the night with her. I daren't trust her alone, and I have to go back to Ruth. I left her without any explanation. I had to make a fast drive to the cottage."

"I can understand that," Jane said.

"Also, I couldn't turn to just anyone for

help," the young doctor went on. "But I know I can trust you. And you and Sally are old acquaintances."

"Surely not friends," Jane said dryly. "I'll stay with her. But I'm doing it only for you. She doesn't deserve any sympathy."

"We turn off the main road soon," he said. And then he peered worriedly into the rear view mirror. "I'd almost swear we were being followed."

Jane glanced around and saw that there was indeed a car close behind them. But there were also several others trailing after it. She turned to the young doctor again and told him, "I don't think you need worry. There are quite a few cars following. It's a heavily traveled road, and they will tailgate."

He nodded. "You're probably right."

"Do we have far to go now?" she asked.

"About a mile or so," he said. "The cottage is on the main road, set in a little."

"Is there a phone?"

"Yes. You can always call me if she gets troublesome."

"I'll want to let my father know I'll be away all night," Jane said. "Otherwise he'll worry."

Wallace Milton gave her a troubled glance. "What will you tell him?"

"That I'm staying with Maggie at her place," she said. "I often have."

"Thanks," the young doctor said gratefully. "I hate involving you in this mess." He slowed the car and turned off the highway onto a gravel roadway. A few yards farther on was the square single-story summer cottage with a light showing in its window.

As they walked toward the front door, he said, "Don't expect Sally to be grateful, but you know I am."

His prediction about the spoiled rich girl proved only too true. Sally was curled up in bed when they went in. She looked pale and ill, but she showed an expression of annoyance as soon as she saw Jane was with young Dr. Milton.

Sitting up in bed, her hair disheveled and her eyes red from crying, she demanded, "What is she doing here?"

"Jane has agreed to stay the night with you," Wallace Milton said firmly.

"I won't have her here!" the blonde girl said petulantly.

"Either that or stay here alone," the young doctor warned her. "You better make up your mind in a hurry."

"I want you to stay," Sally said sullenly.

"I've told you that's impossible. You

need no more medical help. It's just a matter of resting until you're feeling better," he said.

Sally took them both in with a malicious smile. "So this is the way it is," she said with sarcasm. "No wonder you're not interested in me. You already have the head doctor's daughter lined up."

A look of anger darkened Wallace Milton's handsome face. He strode over to the rumpled bed in such a threatening manner that Sally let out a small yelp of alarm as she held the sheets protectively up to her.

"I should slap you hard for saying a thing like that," he threatened. "I want to hear nothing more like it."

The blonde girl began to sniffle. "After I nearly killed myself for you, this is the way you treat me!"

The young doctor sighed and turned to Jane in despair. "You see how it is? Are you still willing to stay with her?"

"Yes," she said. "You go along. We'll make out just fine."

He gave a lingering, disgusted look at the blonde girl in the bed. "I hope so. Phone me if you need me."

Jane closed the door after him and then went back to the living room of the cottage and put a call through to her father. She told him she was staying the night with Maggie. Although he seemed surprised, he accepted the story.

"You'll be going straight to the hospital in the morning then?" he asked.

"Yes. It will save time," she agreed.

"I'll see you then," her father told her. "I'm glad you called."

When she went back into the bedroom, Sally Benson gave her a nasty smile. "I heard you on the phone," she said. "You lied to your father."

"Not for the reason you think," Jane told the other girl.

Sally sneered. "And Steve thinks you're so wonderful! Wait until I tell him about you and Wallace."

"Tell him whatever you like," Jane said coldly. "I'll be sleeping on the cot in the living room. And I'd appreciate your driving me back to town in time for me to report for work in the morning."

"I never get up that early!" the spoiled blonde protested.

Jane smiled wisely. "You will tomorrow."

And she saw to it that the irate Sally did. Jane got up in plenty of time to call her. The cottage was cold in the early morning. But she'd managed a fairly good night's sleep in spite of a poor mattress. Sally grumbled at being wakened so early, but she did get up and dress.

On the way to Whitebridge, the blonde said, "I suppose you're going to spread what I did all around."

"I would as far as you're concerned," she told Sally. "But for Dr. Milton's sake I'm going to say nothing."

"How noble of you!" Sally said mockingly.

Little else was said between them. Sally let Jane out at the hospital, and she went directly to the recreation room and had breakfast before reporting for duty. It wasn't until around ten-thirty that Dr. Wallace Milton came to see his patients and Jane had a few minutes to speak with him privately.

"You managed all right?" the handsome young doctor asked as they stood in the corridor together.

"Yes," she told him. "I even made her get me to work on time."

"Good for you," he said. "I'll be forever grateful to you. Luckily, Ruth didn't ask me too many questions last night. Something new with her."

Jane smiled. "I hope it's a good sign."

"I'd like to believe that," Wallace Milton said seriously. "But I don't dare count on it."

At the first opportunity Jane put through a call to Maggie's house. When she got her friend on the phone, she said, "I stayed at your place last night."

"You did?" Maggie sounded bewildered.

"I did a favor for Dr. Milton and used you as an alibi," she explained. "I had to tell my father something."

"Oh!" Maggie seemed relieved. "Fine. I'll know what to say."

"I thought I'd better let you know as soon as I could," Jane went on. "When will I see you?"

"Maybe tonight," Maggie said. "Boyd and I were going to a drive-in movie. But he's not sure yet. He may have some out-of-town calls to make."

"I'll be home," Jane said. "You can let me know."

"I will," Maggie promised. "I'm anxious to hear what you and Dr. Milton have been up to. I'm sure Sally won't approve."

Jane laughed. "Depend on that!"

Catherine Barton had a new gold-patterned robe and was cutting a dash in the hospital corridors. When Jane met her, the redhead was talking and laughing with Dr. Boyd Davis.

As Jane came up to them, the young Negro doctor told her, "I've been telling

Miss Barton we can use her for the August hospital social. Pretty girls are always in demand."

Jane smiled. "That's true, Catherine. I wasn't sure the socials were still being held."

"They had one last year," Dr. Boyd Davis said. "And they were short of pretty girls for the sales counters."

"Decrepit as I am, I guess I could manage to stand behind a counter a few hours," Catherine said.

"You're bound to be a hit," Jane promised her. "And this year we'll want to raise as much money as possible. The hospital needs it."

"Underline that," Dr. Boyd Davis said wryly.

"Do you always get a good crowd?" Catherine wanted to know.

"We hold the social before the summer people leave," Jane explained. "They are ones we count on for a lot of support."

"Dad and Mother will want to come," Catherine said, her green eyes sparkling with anticipation. "And I'll feel right at home on the hospital grounds. I've been here long enough."

Boyd Davis laughed. "Not much longer, if what I hear is true. I have an idea Dr.

Milton is discharging you tomorrow."

"Really?" Catherine's eyes opened wide. "I must go phone the hotel and let my parents know the good news."

The young Negro doctor raised a warning hand. "Remember, I told you it was a rumor. I can't promise it will happen."

The redhead laughed over her shoulder. "I'll take a chance," she said, and ran off in the direction of her room.

Dr. Davis watched after her and then smiled at Jane. "She's quite a girl."

"She is."

"I'll have a patient coming in this afternoon," he went on. "He'll be in for tests and observation. Has a chronic hoarseness. It has been getting worse. I'm worried it could be a tumor of the larynx."

Jane raised her eyebrows. "A benign tumor?"

"Most of them are," Boyd Davis said. "And where there is a cancerous growth, the cure rate is fairly high. We'll make an examination and send some tissue down to the lab at Bladeworth for a report."

"If it should be cancer, the patient would be better at Bladeworth than here, wouldn't he?" Jane asked frankly.

"That's true," the young Negro doctor

said gravely. "Treatment for cancer of the larynx involves surgery and X-ray irradiation. Since we have no X-ray therapy setup here and Bladeworth does, it would be wiser to send the patient there."

"It will all depend on the biopsy report then."

"Yes," he said, frowning. "I seem to be sending an increasingly large number of my patients to Bladeworth. I suspect it must be annoying to your father."

"Still, he would want them to have the best care."

"I believe that," the young man agreed. "And that is why I have taken this line of action. Of course he's never complained to me. But I know it weakens his arguments on keeping Benson Memorial going."

Jane sighed. "From what I've heard, the council has almost made up its mind about closing us down, though I can't imagine what they'll do with this building if they do."

"That would present a problem," Boyd Davis agreed. "And it's too new a building to abandon."

Jane felt the same way. The knowledge of this gave her a small ray of hope the council might reconsider its stand. And there was old Walter Milligan to offer his voice on Benson Memorial's behalf.

But that very afternoon she met the old man as she was leaving the hospital to get her car in the parking lot. He came shuffling up to her with a smile on his bulldog face.

"Been a few weeks since you had me for a patient," the veteran councilman said.

"So it has," Jane agreed, pausing to talk with him. "How are you feeling?"

He glanced around as if to make sure there was no one overhearing them. Then in a conspiratorial tone, he confessed, "Thirsty!"

Jane laughed. "Why is that?"

"Dr. Milton and your father won't let me touch a drop of booze," the old man said.

"They're right," Jane told him. "You should give yourself a chance."

Walter Milligan regarded the brick hospital building gloomily. "I don't want to find myself in there again."

"Come now," she teased him. "We didn't treat you so badly."

The bulldog face creased in a smile. "Matter of fact, you didn't," he was ready to admit. "I guess maybe I'd be under the green sod if you hadn't taken such good care of me."

"Well, I'm glad to hear you admit it."

"I've told everyone," the veteran councilman assured her. "But the rest of them aren't in a mood to hear either the hospital or your father given too much praise."

"I know."

He shook his head. "What with the school taxes gettin' higher every year, they've got to find a place to cut expenses somewhere. We have only two policemen and a volunteer fire department, so you can't whittle off much in those departments. The one big expense they figure we can do without is Benson Memorial."

"But the trust fund old Mr. Benson left must take care of a lot of our expenses," Jane argued.

"Only about a third of them," Walter Milligan informed her. "The rest the taxpayers have to make up. And come September, I'd say it would all be over. They've been talking to the Benson lawyers."

"And what did they say?"

"It looks like they may be willing to pay the trust fund money to the Bladeworth Hospital to care for patients from Whitebridge. That's what the council has been after. And I think they've finally swung it. It's only a matter of getting a final okay from the lawyers."

Jane's heart sank. She indicated the building. "What do they plan for the hospital itself?"

The old councilman squinted at the solid brick structure. "I've sort of been twitting them about that," he told her. "It's a fine building, and a lot of money has gone into it."

"A good part of which will be completely lost if they decide to use the building for anything but a hospital," she pointed out.

"I told them that, too," Walter Milligan said. "But they're terribly stubborn when they get an idea in their heads."

"I'm sure Steve is for the hospital."

"Yes and no," the old man said. "Like me, he doesn't want to see the money we put into it wasted. But then he agrees with the others that the day has gone when all the little towns like Whitebridge need a hospital. A big complex like they have at Bladeworth is the answer. You can't stop progress, Miss Weaver."

"I'm sure no one wants to," she said. "But in accident cases Bladeworth seems awfully far away. And it's a long way to go to visit someone taking treatment."

"Not with everyone having a car," the old man argued. "It doesn't take anything like the time it would have when Benson

Memorial was built. I'm still on your side, Miss Weaver, but you and your paw have got to see the facts."

"I know that," she agreed.

He eyed the building again. "There's some talk of trying to get a factory in Buffalo to locate a branch plant here. But it's not settled yet."

She managed a forlorn smile. "Then we can still hope."

"And no matter what happens, your dad will always be the best surgeon in these parts. People will want him for a doctor no matter where they go for a hospital."

"But I'm not sure my father would fit in at Bladeworth," she said.

The bulldog face of the veteran councilman smiled encouragingly. "Don't you fret about that, Miss Weaver. A good man like your father fits in anywhere."

She went on to her car with mixed feelings about what Walter Milligan had told her.

As soon as she got home, Aunt Emily told her that Maggie had phoned and asked her to call back. She went into the hallway and dialed her friend at once.

Maggie came on the line and said, "Boyd is tied up tonight, so I'll be free after all."

"Fine," Jane said. "Would you like to come over here?"

"Why don't we go to the drive-in?" Maggie suggested. "It's a picture I'd like to see."

"I don't mind," Jane said. "Will I pick you up?"

"No, we'll use my car," her friend said. "I'll come early, say around eight. The picture won't begin until nine, and that will give us some time to talk."

"I'll be ready," Jane promised.

When she put down the phone and went back to the living room, she found that her father had also arrived home. The aristocratic, white-haired man was standing by the center table with a brief case in his hand. He gave her a searching look.

"You're home early tonight," he observed.

"Yes," she said with a touch of nervousness. "I was just talking to Maggie. We're going to the drive-in together a little later."

"Oh?" He raised his eyebrows. "So you're seeing her again tonight?"

Jane couldn't forget the lie she'd been forced to tell him to protect Wallace Milton. With a forced smile, she said, "We planned it last night in case Boyd should happen to be busy. And he is. So Maggie is free."

188

"Did you have a good time at her place last night?"

"We talked a lot."

Her father smiled thinly. "Female gossip?"

"Sort of."

"In that case, you won't have much to discuss tonight," he suggested.

"We're going mostly to see the show," Jane said quickly. "Maggie had been planning to go with Boyd and doesn't want to miss it."

Her father's eyes met hers. "Jane, why did you deliberately lie to me last night?"

Jane felt her cheeks burn. "What do you mean?"

"Don't go on pretending," her father said sternly. "I happened to stop by Grant's drugstore this morning. And when I mentioned you had stayed with Maggie last night, her father told me I must be mistaken. They were all alone in the house last night."

CHAPTER ELEVEN

Jane smiled bitterly. "I never was a very successful liar, Dad. It's too late for me to begin now. I'm sorry about last night. I had a good reason for telling you what I did. I hope you'll believe that."

Her father's expression was solemn. "You need never lie to me, Jane. Please remember that. Ask me to have faith in you if you like. But don't feel you have to cover up your actions with an untruth."

"I'll remember that," she said quietly.

"See that you do," he told her. "I didn't go around prying and attempting to catch you in a lie. It just happened. When I spoke to Grant, it never occurred to me that you hadn't told the truth."

She felt more unhappy about the unfortunate business than she had before. "I'm sorry, Dad. I had no intention of embarrassing you."

"It would be difficult to embarrass me where an old friend like Grant is concerned. I passed it off by merely saying I thought I must have misunderstood you. But I was fairly sure I hadn't."

"Thanks for covering for me," she said. "I didn't mean to put you in that kind of spot."

"We've discussed it, and now let's forget it," Dr. Graham Weaver said in his brusque way. "I assume you had a good reason for doing what you did. And I also assume there's nothing in this you need to be ashamed of, apart from the lie."

"There isn't, I promise you!"

Her father looked less severe. "As far as I'm concerned, the matter has no more importance." Changing the subject, he said, "I saw you talking to Councilman Milligan just outside the hospital. What did he have to say?"

"Nothing really new," she told him, "except that the council has some kind of offer for the hospital building from a firm in Buffalo."

"They can hardly negotiate to sell it until a decision is made to end our operation," her father said with a touch of anger.

She said, "I suppose they are lining up prospective buyers in case they do decide to shut us off."

"The Benson trust fund people will have something to say about that," her father said. "What they're doing is strictly illegal. They should have permission from the Benson estate before they do any negotiating at all."

"According to the councilman, they have talked with the Benson lawyers and they're awaiting word from them now."

Her father's lined face revealed frustration. "Then I expect the vultures will be moving in on us soon."

They talked no more about it as Aunt Emily summoned them to dinner.

As soon as the meal was over, Jane went upstairs, showered and changed. By the time she came down again in a gray knit suit, Maggie was there to pick her up in the car. As soon as they drove off Jane slumped back against the seat.

"Did I ever get myself in trouble!" she announced.

Maggie smiled from the wheel. "What now?"

Jane told her how her father had dropped by the drugstore and discovered she'd lied. "If only I could tell him the real facts!"

"You can tell me," Maggie said slyly.

Jane gave her friend a resigned smile. "All right; I will." And she did.

They were parked at the drive-in theatre

by the time she had finished. Maggie made a perfect audience, sitting without a word of comment as she heard the whole story.

When Jane ended the account, Maggie shook her head sadly. "That Sally has wound up by getting everyone in trouble."

"She's a silly little beast!" Jane agreed angrily.

"You don't have to tell me," Maggie said. "There wouldn't have been a quarter of the gossip about Boyd Davis and me if she hadn't spread more than her share of vicious lies about us."

"She seems to delight in making people unhappy."

"That's because she's so unhappy herself," Maggie said. "And you'd better watch out what she decides to tell Steve."

"If Steve wants to believe her lies, he can."

"Men have a funny way of jumping to the wrong conclusions," Maggie said. "And I wouldn't want to see anything break you and Steve up again." At this point, their conversation was cut short by the beginning of the movie.

The days of August seemed fairly to skip by. Within another week the August hospital social was due to be held on the grounds. The caretaker was working extra hard preparing the rear gardens and the lawns so they would be at their best. The carpenter was busy in the basement and the shed out back putting the booths together and refurbishing the special decorations of previous years, while the painter added a fresh coat to everything from wheels of fortune to the cloth banner that was strung out over the parking lot announcing the show.

The night before the social, Jane went for a drive and a midnight supper with Steve. She had gone back to the hospital after dinner and spent the entire evening helping the committee decorate the lobby and some of the outside booths. Fair weather had been predicted, and they were putting up the outside tables and booths as early as possible.

Catherine Barton, looking well again, was there to help with the job. She managed to be radiant in the ordinary blue hospital smock she was wearing. Smiling at Jane, she said. "This is the big moment of my vacation, thanks to my still being a partial invalid."

"You'll have fun," Jane promised. "We expect a bumper crowd here, beginning tomorrow afternoon and lasting right through until we close at nine."

She joined the redhead in hanging some balloons along light wires strung between the booths. She was just completing this task when Steve came and picked her up.

"I'm dead tired," she admitted, slumping against the seat back. "But I should have stayed longer."

"Then we'd have had no evening at all," he complained.

"But the social comes only once a year," she reminded him.

"Thank goodness for that," he said, his eyes on the road as they drove along the dark highway to a favorite roadside restaurant. And then, in a different voice, he went on, "Sally came to me with some kind of weird story about you and Wallace Milton."

Jane frowned.

"What kind of story?" she asked.

Steve kept his eyes straight ahead and tried to keep it casual. "You know Sally," he said with attempted lightness. "She always talks in innuendoes and makes you guess a lot as to what she means."

In her weariness, Jane found it easy to be irritable. She said, "Since you're aware of that, I'm surprised you pay any attention to her."

Steve's pleasant face showed chagrin.

"Well," he said, "there is generally at least a kernel of truth in what she says."

"Don't expect me to cheer that sentiment!" Jane said bleakly.

He gave her a quick glance. "Aren't you awfully touchy on the subject?"

"Like most people in Whitebridge, I've had more than I need of your sweet little sister Sally," she said angrily.

"Well, what's this about you and Milton being together at some cottage?"

She stared at him incredulously. "Did she have the nerve to tell you a story like that?"

"Yes."

"If I did happen to have a rendezvous with Dr. Milton, do you think I'd let her know about it?" Jane demanded.

"She said she just happened to drive by. She saw the lights in the cottage and recognized your car."

"And I say it's all her rotten imagination," Jane said. "Now whom do you want to believe?"

It was Steve's turn to be irritable. "I want to believe you, naturally. But I felt I could tell you what she said without your getting angry."

"It's too much to expect," Jane told him, "especially when I'm as beat as I am tonight."

"I'm sorry," he said as he drove up in the parking area before the neon-lit one-story restaurant. And to prove he meant it, he leaned over and kissed her gently before they got out of the car.

So she managed to pass the crisis with Steve without any real harm being done. But she had the feeling the subject might come up again. Sally had aroused Steve's suspicions. Even if he believed the story was exaggerated, he felt there must be some basis for it. Jane had to fight herself to keep from blurting out the true facts.

And she had to battle with herself again the following sunny afternoon when Sally appeared in a ridiculously short mini-dress at the social and had the nerve to smile at her and speak. Jane pretended not to see her and gave her attention to a customer who was selecting some boxed cards from the stand she was supervising.

The social was proving a bigger success than usual. The hospital grounds were crowded, and the lobby was also filled with those who came to enjoy afternoon tea served by the Hospital Ladies' Aid. Those patients who were well enough watched the proceedings from the upper windows of the brick building.

Jane's father moved among the crowds,

greeting old friends and patients and generally acting as host. Dr. Wallace Milton and Dr. Boyd Davis were also spending a couple of hours at the social. All the hospital staff who could be spared were taking part in the gala affair, and there were a lot of volunteer workers.

A quiet voice said, "Good afternoon, Miss Weaver."

Jane glanced up to see Mrs. Davis, Boyd's mother, across the counter from her. The dignified Negro woman had not put in an appearance in Whitebridge since the day she'd visited Jane. According to her son, she now did all her limited shopping in the smaller village of Rangely. So her presence at the social was an event.

Jane smiled at her. "Can I help you?"

The mother of Boyd Davis nodded. "Today you can. I'd like to buy this box of writing paper."

"It's very nice," Jane said approvingly. "And it's only two dollars."

Mrs. Davis handed her two one-dollar bills. "Thank you," she said.

Jane quickly slipped the box of writing paper in a brown paper bag and gave it to the woman. "Your son is here somewhere," she said.

"I know," Mrs. Davis said, her expression inscrutable, as usual. "I don't expect to be staying long. It's been nice seeing you again, Miss Weaver."

"And I've enjoyed seeing you," Jane told her.

The woman merely nodded and went on her way to vanish in the crowd. Jane wondered if she had seen Maggie, who was in charge of a used clothing counter only a short distance away. Probably not. And even if she had, it was unlikely Mrs. Davis would have stopped to speak with her.

Jane saw Mayor Steve Benson and Councilman Walter Milligan standing on the outer edge of the thronging crowd. Steve waved to her and smiled, and she waved back. Then she saw Dr. Wallace Milton pushing his way through the clusters of people to reach her stand.

He came up and joined her behind the counter. "Well," he said with a deep sigh, "at least I've found one place to retreat."

She laughed. "Is it that bad?"

He shook his head. "You have no idea! Everyone out there seems to have been a patient of mine. And they all expect me to remember every detail of their illnesses. Most of them are just blurs to me."

"Dad has the same problems every year."

"This is only my second social," the handsome young doctor said, "and I hope it's my last."

"It's liable to be if the hospital closes," she reminded him as she moved away to wait on a customer.

Wallace Milton continued to stand at the other end of her counter. When she finished giving the customer the cards she'd bought and the proper change, Jane looked up to see her father and Dr. Boyd Davis standing by Maggie's counter talking to her.

She was about to rejoin Dr. Milton when a woman's figure emerged from the crowd and came directly over to the counter. It was Ruth Milton! Jane took one glance at the angry face of the young doctor's wife and knew there was a scene in the making. Ruth was dressed in an untidy, frantic fashion. Her hair was only roughly combed, and her make-up was uneven and glaring. She looked the mental case she was.

Glaring at them as they stood in surprised dismay behind the counter, Ruth Milton fairly screamed, "So you're with her again!"

Her husband was already on his way to try to placate her, saying, "Please, Ruth! You're confused!"

A hush had fallen over the crowd as they watched the unexpected show. Ruth pulled away from her husband's grasp. "Don't think I've been fooled," she shouted hysterically. "I saw you at the cottage. I followed you two there in my car that night!"

Jane listened in horror as the woman's words carried to everyone on the hospital grounds. She remembered the car that had been behind them the night she'd gone to stay with Sally. Wallace Milton had been right in his hunch, although they'd not guessed who was in the car trailing them.

Once again the young doctor tried to grasp the hysterical Ruth and placate her. "Please, Ruth!" he begged.

"Stay with her!" his wife jeered in a loud voice. "I don't want any part of you!" And with that she ran off through the crowd, elbowing her way and disappearing in a moment.

Dr. Wallace Milton lingered long enough to offer Jane a despairing glance. "I'm sorry," he said. And then he hurried off to try to catch up with the wildly fleeing Ruth.

The next person to join Jane was her father. His aristocratic face was flushed, and in a low, urgent voice he said, "You can't stay here. Come with me to my office."

She gestured toward the counter. "What about these things?"

Her father's hand was gripping her arm. "Dr. Davis will appoint somebody to take care of your counter," he told her, and led her to the side door of the hospital, using a back way at the rear of the stands.

As they went inside Jane could hear the sound system with its band records had been turned up. She looked back and saw that the shocked bystanders were moving about again.

Jane and her father quickly walked down the long corridor to his office. When they were inside and the door closed, he turned to her. "What did that scene mean?" he demanded.

"You know she's not responsible," Jane faltered. "She should be in an institution."

"I haven't time to discuss that now," her father said. "I heard the accusation she made in front of most of the town. And I want you to explain."

Jane shook her head miserably. "She got everything wrong, Dad!"

"Suppose you tell it to me," he suggested.

She saw that it couldn't be put off any longer. There was no need to worry about protecting Wallace Milton after what had gone on. And Sally deserved to be exposed.

"It happened the evening I was out all night," she began. "The night I said I was at Maggie's."

"Go on."

She told him the whole story quickly. "I meant to tell you sometime. But I didn't expect anything like this would happen before I had the chance," she finished.

Her father stared at her for a long moment of silence. Then he brushed his hand across his forehead. "It won't be easy to explain to all those people who heard Ruth Milton screaming at you," he said.

Jane felt differently about it now that she'd told her father the truth. "I really don't care," she said. "If they're so small-minded they'll take a mentally ill woman's words seriously, then it doesn't matter!"

"I'm glad you feel that way," her father said. "I'm not sure I do."

There was a knock on the office door. He went over and opened it. Steve was standing there with a stern look on his face. Jane's father said, "Well?"

"I don't want to interrupt," Steve said. "But I would like to speak to Jane a minute."

Jane's father stood with his hand on the doorknob. "You heard what went on out there a while ago?" he asked Steve.

Steve nodded. "Yes. That's why I want to talk to Jane."

Not knowing what he might have to say, Jane stepped over to her father's side. Facing Steve, she said, "What do you have to tell me?"

The young mayor of Whitebridge took a step into the office so that he was close to her. "After what Ruth said, I located Sally. I didn't let her go until she told me the truth." He glanced toward her father. "Do you know what really happened, Doctor?"

Her father nodded. "Yes. Jane has just told me. A little late, but she's given me the whole story."

Steve regarded her unhappily. "I'm sorry, Jane. I doubt if we can expect my sister to confess the truth to anyone else. But at least I made her tell me."

"It's all right," Jane said dully. So much had happened in such a short time she'd had no chance to evaluate where it left her.

She heard her father saying, "Jane wants to go back and look after her counter."

"I think she should," Steve agreed. "Not many people heard what Ruth actually said. And most of them know she's had a breakdown. It would look worse if Jane ran out on the social."

"You're probably right," her father said, and turned to her. "Do you still feel up to it?"

"I think so," she said.

"Very well; I'll go with you," her father said firmly.

Steve nodded. "And just to show solidarity, I'll go behind the counter and work with you."

Jane managed a forlorn smile. "I hadn't expected any offers like that."

The three of them were on their way back to the counter when Dr. Boyd Davis came hurrying to meet them. One glance at the young Negro doctor's drawn face told Jane there was more bad news.

As he met them, he said, "There's been an accident! Ruth Milton's car went over the embankment by the river! She's alive but in serious condition. A police car is bringing her back to the hospital now."

He'd barely finished speaking when the harsh scream of an approaching siren came to them above the sounds of the social.

CHAPTER TWELVE

So it came about that within an hour of the time when Ruth Milton had stood hysterically hurling accusations at Jane across the counter at the social, Jane found herself standing over the draped body of the young doctor's wife in the operating room of Benson Memorial. Ruth Milton had been brought in suffering from a fracture of her left leg, possible internal injuries and, worst of all, serious head injuries.

From the moment she'd arrived in the emergency room there had been no question but that an operation would be required at once to ease the pressure of the head injuries. The injured woman was alive but just barely. A pale and stricken Wallace Milton joined Jane's father and Dr. Boyd Davis in an examination of Ruth.

Dr. Weaver's troubled face reflected his pessimism about the chances of survival of his colleague's wife. He said, "There's only one course. We must operate at once."

Wallace Milton nodded. "No time to

send her to Bladeworth," he murmured.

"I'm afraid not," Jane's father agreed, "though they are better set up for this type of surgery. It's one of those emergencies we're always talking about."

Wallace Milton was visibly trembling. "Let's lose no time then," he said.

Jane's father touched the arm of the shaken man. "There's no question of you being in on this. Dr. Davis and I will manage. Miss McCumber is here, and we can have her look after the anesthesia. Jane will supervise the nursing end and scrub for us."

The young doctor offered no objections. His attempt to catch up with his wife's careening car had ended with him witnessing the climactic tragedy from the wheel of his own car. The ordeal had left him in a state of almost complete collapse.

For Jane and the others, the brisk orders of the head surgeon had been a signal for hurried preparations. Outside the hospital the August social went on, although the gaiety of the occasion had been ruined by the tragedy of Ruth Milton's accident. The full extent of her injuries had not been revealed, and so they were not aware of the life and death struggle taking place indoors.

It was a solemn group of white-masked figures who gathered around the brightly lighted operating table on which Ruth Milton was stretched out under sterile drapes. Jane had shaved the damaged head area as well as she could and cleansed the frightening portion of crushed skull. Only the area to be operated on was exposed.

Dr. Graham Weaver began the intricate business of relieving the dangerous pressure and removing the threatening bone splinters. Jane had never seen him work so deftly and yet with such care. And Dr. Boyd Davis revealed himself in a new light as he skillfully aided her father. The strain this unfamiliar task exerted on him was revealed by the copious perspiration streaming down his dark temples and cheeks. The circulating nurse again and again touched a towel to the perspiring areas.

An hour passed, and they were still caught up in the awesome task of trying to save Ruth Milton. Care had to be exercised not to damage any normal brain tissue and to minimize the loss of blood. Then there came a tense moment when it seemed the weak beat of the patient's heart had ceased altogether.

Miss McCumber's eyes were frantic behind her glasses as she groped at the controls of the anesthesia machine in response to curt orders from Jane's father. Then Ruth's heartbeat became more normal and the operation continued.

More than two hours had elapsed before Ruth was wheeled out, the emergency surgery completed. Jane's father took off his mask and told Dr. Boyd Davis, "We daren't leave her alone. One or the other of us should be with her during the next few hours."

The young Negro doctor nodded. "Yes, sir. Shall I take the first turn?"

Jane's father considered. "Probably you'd better," he said. "It will give me a chance to go back outside. I'll mingle with the people and try to ease some of the tension all this must have induced." He frowned. "We'll want to cut down on that public address system music and keep other noise to a minimum."

Jane and the nurse who'd been summoned to assist her began the cleaning up of the operating room, with the help of Miss McCumber. The stout head nurse had been serving tea until she'd been called to assist with the surgery.

Now she paused to tell Jane, "I just can't go back down there and pour tea and coffee and make a lot of bright remarks in the state I'm in now."

"I don't think you need worry," Jane said. "That part of the social will have ended."

"So it will," Miss McCumber said, glancing at the wall clock and seeing that it was nearly eight. "The social is due to end in an hour, and I imagine after what's happened, most of them will have left anyway."

"You're probably right," Jane agreed.

"What could have gotten into that woman to do such a thing?" the head nurse wanted to know.

"It's been building for a long time," Jane said. "Something awful was bound to happen."

When she finished in the operating room, she went back to her father's office and found Wallace Milton there alone. He still looked white and ill as he paced up and down. He halted when she came in and stared at her with frightened eyes.

She guessed his fears and quickly said, "I have no news. Where is Dad?"

"He's gone up to be with Ruth," the young doctor said, his face grim. "I just left there. She's not responding."

"She was hurt very badly," Jane said quietly.

"I know," he agreed. "It's too much to expect she'll recover. But I can't help hoping."

"You should," she agreed. "There's always a chance as long as there's life."

But Ruth Milton's life was even then limited to only a few minutes longer. Jane was still in the office with Wallace Milton when she saw her father and Boyd Davis come to the open doorway and hesitate. The expression on their faces and the fact that neither of them were with the patient told her without need of words that Ruth had died.

After that events happened at a frantic pace. The days before and after the funeral of the young doctor's wife would always remain clouded in Jane's memory. Yet she responded to the needs of the moment in an almost automatic fashion without really comprehending what was going on. Yet one thing was clear in her mind. Ruth's tragic death had marked a turning point. And it would mean vast changes in most of their lives.

It was the death knell for Benson Memorial. When the council met early in September, they quickly decided to cease the operations of the institution and turn the money over to the Bladeworth Hospital for the benefit of the local people. The Benson executors had decided this was reasonably carrying out the intentions of the trust fund.

Walter Milligan argued briefly on behalf of Jane's father and the hospital remaining as it was. But he lost out. The theory that there was need of a local operating room for emergencies had been given a bad blow by Ruth's death after her emergency operation. It wasn't a typical case, as Jane's father pointed out. But it was one that had gotten a lot of publicity and served well for the purpose of proving that Bladeworth's emergency room was near enough.

Dr. Wallace Milton remained in the area only long enough to wind up his practice and turn his patients over to Dr. Boyd Davis. Then he left to take a month's rest visiting relatives in Washington.

Jane's father had accepted the closing of his be-loved hospital in tight-lipped fashion. He said little but went on with his day-to-day routine as if there were going to be no changes. But come January first, Benson Memorial's doors would be closed. He had received a tentative offer from the Bladeworth Hospital, but Jane knew he had done nothing about it.

Aunt Emily was in a perturbed state about the turn of events. "Your father has never looked worse," she told Jane. "He's not eating anything at all, and I can see him aging every day."

"It's taking him time to adjust to the idea," Jane had said.

Aunt Emily's plain face showed scorn. "Adjust! Can you see him doing it? Can you think of him without Benson Memorial? And can you imagine the hospital as some factory or whatever they're trying to sell it for?"

Jane had not been able to make any satisfactory answer. Aunt Emily had pictured the situation only too clearly. She couldn't see her father carrying on once he was deprived of the hospital's facilities. And yet it was something he must do.

She went to the hotel to see Catherine Barton before the redhead and her parents left Whitebridge at the end of September. The extra weeks had worked wonders for the attractive girl.

As they were saying goodbye on the hotel steps, Catherine said, "In spite of all that happened, I'm not sorry I came to Whitebridge this summer."

"You're riding again, so the fall didn't frighten you," Jane observed.

"Not a bit," Catherine agreed. "And

didn't it bring me a handsome doctor, although I've lost him now?"

"There are others beside you who are mourning Dr. Wallace Milton's departure," Jane said. "Sally Benson for one. She made an awful scene because he refused to see her before he left."

"That one!" Catherine said with disgust on her lovely face. "She caused all the trouble."

"She certainly did her share," Jane agreed.

"Well, Dr. Milton was more considerate of me than he was of her." Catherine smiled. "He did come to say goodbye before he left."

"Why not?" Jane said. "You were one of his prize patients."

"I certainly hope so," Catherine said. "And what about you? Will you be here when we come back to the hotel next season?"

Jane smiled. "That's hard to tell. You know the hospital is closing."

"Yes. I think that's too bad."

"So do I," Jane said. "It will mean a drastic change for my father. It's one of the main reasons I came back. Now I don't know what I'll do."

Catherine gave her a wise look. "Maybe

Steve Benson will decide for you."

Jane shrugged. "He's offered to. But I can't see myself as the mayor's wife in this small town. Perhaps I'm a career girl at heart. My nursing means a lot to me. I enjoyed the challenge of my work in Boston."

"So you may go back there?"

"Perhaps," Jane said with a sigh. "I do like Steve. It's a hard decision."

"I wish you luck whatever you do," Catherine said with sincerity. "And I hope we all meet again next year."

Jane hoped so as well. But she doubted that they would. With the loss of the summer visitors, the pace at the hospital slowed down. The news of its closing also had an effect on those requiring hospitalization, many of them deciding to go to Bladeworth. The nursing staff was cut to a minimum, with only herself, Miss McCumber and one other registered nurse remaining.

Then, in late October, she learned of another impending change in the pattern of life in Whitebridge. Maggie Grant invited her over for dinner. And when she got there Dr. Boyd Davis was also a dinner guest. Maggie's father was absent, as he was doing evening duty at the drugstore and took his meal there. At once Jane received the impression Maggie and Boyd had something important to tell her.

Yet they discussed only casual everyday things until they left the table to gather in the living room around the fireplace and have their after-dinner coffee. Dr. Boyd Davis stood by the fireplace, the reflection from the blazing log fire Maggie had started against the chill of the night high-lighting his handsome ebony-colored face. The two girls sat together on a davenport facing him and the fireplace.

Maggie smiled at Jane over her coffee cup. "I suppose you've guessed we have some news."

Jane nodded. "Yes."

Maggie glanced up at Boyd Davis. "I think you should tell her, Boyd."

The young Negro doctor lifted his eye-brows. "If you say so. Well, Jane, Maggie and I are announcing our engagement."

"Congratulations," Jane said. "I wish you every happiness."

"I know you do," Boyd said. "But that's not all of it. We don't plan to be married for at least a year."

Jane glanced at Maggie. "Why the delay?"

"Boyd is taking on a new job, for one thing," her friend said.

This was another surprise. Jane looked up at the young doctor. "Does Dad know about this yet?"

He shook his head. "No. I think he has enough problems of his own. But I plan to tell him in a few days."

Jane frowned. "It's going to leave the area very short of doctors."

"Not really," he said. "We are rushed only during the holiday season when the summer people are here. The rest of the year, one doctor can handle things easily. And I assume your father will be remaining, even though the hospital is going to close."

"I suppose so," Jane said rather forlornly. "Nothing seems to be remaining the same any more."

Boyd Davis said, "I have the offer of a research job in Philadelphia. It's a field in which I have training and which interests me. I probably can offer more to my profession in research than I ever could as a general practitioner."

Jane smiled. "I'm sure Dad will be proud you've been offered this position. He's always felt you had a special talent."

Boyd Davis spoke earnestly, "And I would not have wanted to miss the opportunity of working here with him. I've learned a great deal, about human nature as well as medicine. Another reason for my wanting to take a research post is that I believe it will be fairer to Maggie when we are married. We can have more privacy and security. At this stage of development in racial adjustment, public life does not offer the best opportunity for a mixed marriage."

"I don't think you'll face many problems," Jane said.

"Boyd disagrees," Maggie told her. "And he's probably right. And as long as we're giving out news bulletins, I may as well tell you I'm leaving the first of the year."

"Leaving Whitebridge?" Jane said. "What about your teaching?"

Boyd Davis spoke up, "She's going to continue teaching. Only it will be in a Negro school in the Deep South. She'll be working for a special foundation among underprivileged children." He paused to smile. "I want her to see how it is with my people. I don't want her to rush into marriage with me, thinking every Negro is an educated professional and the integration problem is cosily looking after itself. Nor do I want her to be a cocktail party liberal with uplifting ideas about improving the black people's lot and no real knowledge of what the problem is about. After she's taught a year among poor Negroes, she'll know my people and me better. She can decide then whether she wants to go through with our marriage or not."

Maggie looked up at him with adoring eyes. "You needn't worry about that. You won't get rid of me."

He laughed easily. "And I don't want to. But it has to be a marriage based on honesty. This is the one way I know to try to attempt that. What do you think, Jane?" He turned to her.

"I think you'll both manage very well," was her verdict. And she really believed it.

Her father was actually pleased when he heard Boyd Davis had been tendered an important research job. "He would be a fool not to accept it," was his comment. "He's too important a talent to bury himself in a small-town practice."

Jane reproached her father, saying, "I hope that's not the way you feel about your own career. You've done wonderful work in this remote country."

"I represent different times and a different talent," her father said with a sad smile on his aristocratic features. "I'm outdated already. In an age when diagnosis is being conducted on closed circuit television with the patient in one city and the doctor in another, the horse and buggy practitioner will soon be a curiosity. Bladeworth Hospital has a computer system that will eventually take care of all the initial interviews of every patient admitted."

It gave her an opportunity to ask an important question. "What about Bladeworth, Dad? Have you decided to join their staff?"

He looked unhappy. "Not yet. Plenty of time for that," he said, evading any direct reply.

The first snow arrived early in November. And with it came a letter from Virginia from Catherine Barton, informing Jane that she had found an ideal man and hoped to be married soon. The lovely redhead didn't say who the man was or when the marriage would take place. Jane wrote her an immediate reply and congratulated her.

It seemed to be a time for offering congratulations. Yet she was not in line for any. Of course that was her own fault. Steve Benson had not given up asking her to marry him. In fact, lately he had been more insistent than ever.

"Everyone we know is getting married," he complained humorously one night in

November when he came to call on her. "Even Sally has come up with some boob of a New Yorker who is willing to make her his wife."

Jane smiled. "It may be the thing she needs." They were sitting on the divan in the living room. Aunt Emily was upstairs with her television set and Jane's father was attending a council meeting concerning the winding up of the hospital's affairs.

Steve looked skeptical. "I doubt if anything will change Sally," he said. "She still feels pretty blue about losing Dr. Milton, but she seems ready to decide on this other fellow on the rebound."

"So you'll be alone with your mother," Jane said.

"Mother leaves for Florida for the winter right after Christmas," Steve said. "So I'll be alone, period." He stared at her earnestly. "Why can't you make up your mind about us?"

"Things are so mixed up for me," she pleaded. "Give me a little more time."

"Is it because your marriage went sour? You've grieved enough, if that's the case. Give me a chance to show you what a good marriage can be."

She put her hand on his and studied him

fondly. "I wish I could say yes, Steve. I really do."

His good night kiss was as warm as usual. But she watched him drive away with a sudden depressed feeling that she was going to lose him. Because she couldn't make up her mind, it was inevitable they would drift apart. She hadn't a right to expect anything else.

Still, she couldn't see a future for her in Whitebridge. She felt reasonably sure she loved Steve, and it would be painful to break with him. But she did not want to make another mistake in marriage. And she was badly worried about her father and what he was going to do.

Things were very slow at the hospital. The melancholy task of preparing lists of equipment that would be offered for sale was under way. Only about a dozen patients were being treated on the average. They had done little operating, and her father seemed older and less interested in the world around him each day.

On a bleak afternoon in early December, Jane went downstairs to the desk in the lobby to ask Daisy to pass on a message to the relative of a patient.

Daisy was busy at the switchboard, and so Jane went over to the entrance doors to look out as she waited. A light snow was falling, and there had been the warning of a storm by early evening.

As she stood there looking out, a dark sedan drove up. And when the driver got out and came toward the front steps, she at once recognized the slim figure in top-coat and soft black hat as Dr. Wallace Milton.

She gave a small gasp of pleased surprise, and when he came in to face her, she said, "You're the last one I was expecting to see!"

The handsome young doctor smiled and said, "I drove up from Boston. I've been trying to beat the storm here."

"And you've managed it," she said. "You look well!"

"I feel fine," he told her. "Where is your father?"

"In his office," she said. "We're not too busy, since it's nearly time to close. There are only ten patients registered today."

He showed mild astonishment. "That's really low," he agreed. "Well, show me to your dad. I'd like to talk to both of you."

Jane's father treated the young doctor like a returned prodigal. Jane remained for a few minutes at the request of both men. Her father regarded Wallace Milton with interest and said, "What brings you back here?"

"Medicine," was his surprising answer. "While I was in Washington, I was offered a federal job, and I accepted it. Ever hear of the new department that has been set up to establish experimental homes for geriatric care? It's known as Homes For the Aged; in Washington parlance, HFTA."

Her father considered. "It sounds faintly familiar."

"There have been references to it in the various medical journals," Dr. Milton went on. "We're just getting started. The idea is to set up a number of small convalescent hospitals in various areas of the country to fix standards and find out the proper answers to the care of the aging sick." He paused significantly. "I understand Benson Memorial is still for sale."

"It is," her father agreed.

"I have been authorized by the government to make an offer for it," Wallace Milton went on with a smile. "We'd like to make it one of our test units. And we'd be especially pleased if you would agree to remain on as director — it needn't interfere with your private practice — and head the local staff."

Jane could hardly believe the good news.

It was such a wonderful offer it exceeded any hopes for a miracle she might have had. One glance at the radiant smile on her father's face told her how he felt.

"That sounds mighty interesting," he said softly. "I just may take you up on it."

The early stages of the deal were verbally settled before Wallace Milton left the office. A quick call on the phone to Steve Benson revealed the council would be all for the plan. And at Dr. Milton's suggestion, Steve agreed to come over. Jane's father went out to get some records, leaving them alone.

While they were waiting for Steve, the handsome young doctor turned his attention to her. "What's happening in your life, Jane?" he asked.

She blushed. "Not much. The offer you've brought is the best thing."

"I mean on a personal basis," he said. "I'm beginning to pick up the threads of my own life. It will take a while, but the prospects are good." He hesitated significantly. "By the way, you remember Catherine Barton?"

"Yes."

"She lives in Virginia close to Washington. We've been seeing each other fairly often. And it's likely we'll be making plans for an autumn wedding."

Jane recalled Catherine's letter. She'd never guessed that Wallace Milton was the mystery man. She said, "She told me, but she didn't say who it was."

He smiled. "Now you know. But why haven't you married Steve?"

She showed a rueful expression. "It's a long story."

"I think I can guess," the young doctor said. "It's partly that first mistake, partly concern for your father, and mostly the tug between your love for nursing and your love for Steve."

Jane smiled in surprise. "How could you come so close?"

He was on his feet facing her. "Well, I've solved the difficulty about your father; let's see what else I can do."

They were interrupted by Jane's father returning with Steve. Steve had his overcoat on his arm as he shook hands with Wallace Milton. He said, "You're really doing Whitebridge a favor, Doctor."

Wallace Milton's eyes held a twinkle. "And now maybe I can do one for you and Jane. We'd very much like an experienced registered nurse to supervise our nursing staff; someone who could carry on a couple of years full time and then maybe continue on a part-time basis." He winked at Steve. "My idea of the perfect sort of girl for the job would be the mayor's wife."

Steve's pleased expression showed he'd gotten the message. He glanced Jane's way. "Great idea," he agreed. "The only trouble is that I happen to be a bachelor. Now if I could meet the right girl —"

Jane laughed. "Look no further," she said, going to his arms.

And so it was settled then and there in the prosaic setting of her father's office. She and Steve kissed while the other two looked on and smiled their approval. Again her final decision had been wildly impulsive. But this time she knew it would be all right.

We hope you have enjoyed this Large Print book. Other Thorndike, Wheeler or Chivers Press Large Print books are available at your library or directly from the publishers.

For more information about current and upcoming titles, please call or write, without obligation, to:

Publisher
Thorndike Press
295 Kennedy Memorial Drive
Waterville, ME   04901
Tel. (800) 223-1244

Or visit our Web site at:
www.gale.com/thorndike
www.gale.com/wheeler

OR

Chivers Large Print
published by BBC Audiobooks Ltd
St James House, The Square
Lower Bristol Road
Bath BA2 3SB
England
Tel. +44(0) 800 136919
email: bbcaudiobooks@bbc.co.uk
www.bbcaudiobooks.co.uk

All our Large Print titles are designed for easy reading, and all our books are made to last.